ADVENTURES OF THE

GREEK HEROES

ADVENTURES
❦ OF THE ❦
GREEK HEROES

MOLLIE McLEAN & ANNE WISEMAN

Illustrated by Witold T. Mars

HOUGHTON MIFFLIN COMPANY   BOSTON

PUBLISHED BY HOUGHTON MIFFLIN COMPANY, DISTRIBUTED TO THE
SCHOOLS BY XEROX EDUCATION PUBLICATIONS
COPYRIGHT © 1961 BY MOLLIE MCLEAN AND ANNE M. WISEMAN
COPYRIGHT © RENEWED 1989 BY ANNE WISEMAN

RNF ISBN 0-395-06913-0   PAP ISBN 0-395-13714-4
LIBRARY OF CONGRESS CATALOG CARD NUMBER: 61–10628

Printed in the United States of America

VB   30

❧ CONTENTS ❧

MANY YEARS AGO, there lived a people called the Greeks. You will enjoy reading about them because they, like we, loved games and contests of all kinds. They were good at many things. They liked games of running and jumping. They liked to box and to wrestle. They liked to race their horses, and they were good at using the sword. It is said that some of them could throw a spear better than any other people of that time.

The Greeks were not only strong, they were good thinkers, too. They liked to write music and make poems. Sometimes they put the music and poems together to make plays.

Every five years, at a little town called Olympia, the Greeks held a great contest to find out who were the strongest men in all Greece and who were the greatest thinkers. Men and boys from all of Greece came to be in the games. People from every land came to see them. First the contests of running, jumping, and throwing the spear were held. Then came the games of boxing and wrestling. Then the men raced their horses against one another. The winner was given a prize. He became a hero and his name was known all over the world. Last, the contests were held to see who was the best writer of music and poetry. It may seem to you that these contests could not have been as much fun as the contests of running and jumping, but the Greek people liked them almost the best of all. The winners of the prizes for the poems were as great heroes as the winners of the games of running and jumping. What did the poets tell about that made the Greek people like them so much? What stories did they tell that made the people listen without a sound?

The stories in this book are the stories those Greek poets told at Olympia. They are the stories of the first Greek heroes. You will read of strong Hercules, who killed a three-headed monster. You will read of brave Perseus, who killed the giant Atlas. You will read of fierce Theseus and his fight with a cruel monster called the Minotaur. You will read about other heroes — Orpheus, Meleager, and Jason. Then you will read a story in which all the heroes go together on a brave adventure.

These are the stories which the Greek poets told at Olympia. May you enjoy them as they did.

HERCULES

HERCULES
⚘ AND ⚘
PROMETHEUS

1

FIRST OF ALL the heroes that the poets told about was strong Hercules. He was the son of Zeus, who was king of the Greek gods. One of the stories told about Hercules was that when he was a little child two giant snakes had tried to kill him. Most babies would have been afraid, but Hercules was not. He held the snakes away from him and, with his two small hands, killed them.

As Hercules grew older, he became more and more powerful. He could do things which no other man could do. He could have used his power to hurt others, but he was kind and good. He went about the world helping people who were not as strong as he.

The first man Hercules helped was Prometheus. This is the way the story was told.

There were many Greek gods. Zeus, their king, was the most powerful of all. At one time, he called all the gods and goddesses to a meeting at his palace on Mount Olympus. They came as fast as they could because they heard that Zeus was angry. When he came before them, he had a fierce look on his face.

"I am not pleased with the kingdom of Man," roared Zeus. "Men forget their gods, and use their time looking for riches."

The gods and goddesses were angry when they heard this. They had given Man many gifts and did not want the people of the world to forget them.

"What shall we do to make Man more thankful for the things he has been given?" asked Diana, goddess of the moon.

"We shall take away one of the gifts he uses the most," answered Zeus.

The gods and goddesses began to think of the gifts they had given the world.

"We could take back my gift," said beautiful Diana. "Without my light the people would

find the nights very black."

"The moon is very pretty, but men do not use it much," said Neptune, god of the sea. "They would not miss your gift as they would mine. Were the sea to dry up, men would be very unhappy."

"You are right," said Apollo, god of the sun, "but think of what the world would be like without my gift. There would be no daylight. Trees and flowers would not grow. The world would be cold. No one could live without the sun."

"Apollo forgets one thing," said Zeus. "I do not want to kill the people of the world. I only wish to teach them a lesson. If we took the sun from Man, he would soon die."

"There is one thing we can take away from Man which he will miss very much," said Vulcan. "Let us take away my gift, fire. Without it, he will be unhappy, but he will not die."

"Good!" roared Zeus. "It shall be as you have said, Vulcan. From this day on, there will be no fire for men."

As he said this, the warm day became cold and black. A strong wind shook the trees. All the fires on earth began to go out. Soon only one was left. This, Zeus put in a hollow tube which he carried back to Mount Olympus.

"Now," said Zeus fiercely. "I shall keep this

hollow tube with me always. Man will never have fire again."

After Zeus took fire away, the world was sad. When the sun went down, there was no light. Men could not find their way. Many people were lost in the black night. There was no fire to warm the people. They would try to sleep and forget how cold they were. There was no cooking. Men would bring home animals which they had killed, only to find they must eat them as they were. They remembered the feasts they had had before.

Now fierce monsters who once had been afraid of the fire carried off sheep, chickens, and cows. Sometimes they even took a little child.

Year by year, the people of the world became more unhappy. Over and over again they asked Zeus to give them back the gift of fire. They said they would not forget the gods again. They said that they would thank the gods every day for the many gifts they had been given.

The gods and goddesses did not think Zeus should keep fire from Man for so long a time. They wanted people to be happy again. They asked Zeus to give fire back to the world.

Zeus roared, "I am the king of the gods. I took fire from Man and I will give it back when I wish."

The gods and goddesses could not make Zeus forget his anger. But they did not like to look down on a world so cold and black.

When the people of the world found that Zeus would not forget, they called a meeting. They met in an underground cave where the farseeing eyes of Zeus could not find them. They said how unhappy they were without fire. They said that they had done everything they could to please Zeus but that he would not give fire back to them.

"We must find a way to take fire back from Zeus," said one man.

"Yes," said another. "We cannot live without it any longer."

"Who would be so brave as to try to take something from the king of the gods?" asked a girl.

The people looked at one another. Their faces were sad. Every man wanted to help the world, but none was brave enough.

All at once a man stood up in the crowd.

"I will steal the fire from Zeus," he said.

Everyone at the meeting looked at him.

Then a man asked, "Who are you?"

All the people shouted, "Yes, tell us your name!"

"I am Prometheus," he said.

"I have heard of you," one man said, "and I know you are brave. But how will you take fire from Zeus? The king of the gods can see all the world from where he sits. You could not steal it, for he would see you."

Prometheus gave a laugh and said, "He can see nothing when he sleeps! I shall steal it at night."

The people looked at one another. They had not known there was so brave a man in all the world.

"When will you go?" they asked.

"I shall go now," said Prometheus. He put on his sword and walked out into the black night.

As Prometheus came near Mount Olympus, he heard the gods and goddesses laughing and singing. He saw the bright palace of Zeus where all had come to eat and drink. He heard fierce

Zeus telling the story of how he had taken fire
from Man. He saw the king of the gods laugh as
he held over his head the hollow tube in which
he had put the fire. As Zeus laughed, the walls

of the palace shook, but Prometheus was not afraid.

For a long time Prometheus watched the bright windows of the palace. At last, one by one, the lights went out as the gods and goddesses went home. All was dark. Prometheus knew his time had come. Quietly, he opened the golden door of the palace. Without a sound he walked to the room where the king of the gods was sleeping. He saw the hollow tube in which Zeus had put the fire. He picked it up. Just then, powerful Zeus turned over. Prometheus jumped back and, still holding the hollow tube, put his hand on his sword. He stood quietly watching. Soon Zeus was sleeping soundly again. Prometheus ran from the palace, the hollow tube in his hand. When he reached the earth, he gave fire to everyone. The night which had been black was bright, and once again the world was happy.

2

IN THE MORNING Zeus found that the hollow tube was gone. His anger was so great that even Mount Olympus shook. He sent his messenger,

Mercury, to earth to find out who had taken the fire. Mercury came back and said, "A man named Prometheus came in the night and took the fire back to earth."

"Who is this Prometheus that steals from the gods?" roared Zeus. "Bring him here at once!"

Mercury went back to earth as fast as he could. Soon Prometheus was standing before the king of the gods. Zeus looked hard at him. "Did you think you could steal from me, little man," he said. As he spoke, the ground shook and the sky grew black. "I will teach you not to steal from the king of the gods," he roared.

"I am not afraid," said Prometheus. "I would steal from you again to help Man. It was not right to keep fire from him so long."

"You will never steal from anyone again," shouted Zeus. He pulled Prometheus to the window of the palace. From there they could see the whole world.

"Look down, little man," he said. "Do you see that far-off rock that overlooks the angry sea? That will be your home until the world ends."

The king of the gods went to another room

in the palace and came back carrying an ugly black vulture.

"This bird will be your guard. He will watch you day and night." Zeus turned to Mercury and said, "Take this man to the place I have shown you. Chain him to the rock so he cannot move. Let the vulture fly around him." Turning to Prometheus he said, "Now, little man, we will see how brave you are." He gave a cruel laugh and left the room.

Mercury took Prometheus to the far-off place. He chained him to the rock. Leaving the vulture to guard him, he went back to Olympus.

For many years Prometheus stayed chained to the rock. In the day, the hot sun beat down on him. At night, the cold rain fell on him. All he could hear was the roaring of the wind and sea. All he could see was the ugly black bird flying around him. No one came near him. The people of the world wanted to help, but they were afraid of the anger of Zeus.

Prometheus did not like being chained to the rock, but he was happy that he had taken the fire from Zeus. He knew he had helped the people of the world. Also he had a secret which he

had not told Zeus. He knew that one day a great
hero would come to save him. He did not know
the name of the hero or when he would come.
All he knew was that one day he would be saved
by a strong and powerful man. Prometheus
looked for the hero every day.

One morning Prometheus saw a white sail far
out on the angry sea. As it came nearer, he saw

a powerful man jump from the boat and swim to the rock.

"Are you the hero who has come to save me?" shouted Prometheus.

"I am Hercules," the man shouted back. "I have come to save you because you helped the people of the world."

As Hercules came out of the water, Prometheus could see he was more powerful than other men. He was very tall, and his arms were strong. In his hands he carried a great sword. With one jump he landed on the rock.

"Watch out for the vulture which guards me," shouted Prometheus. "He will try to kill you."

"Let him try," laughed the hero as the vulture flew at him. With his giant sword he cut off the head of the ugly bird.

Hercules turned to Prometheus. With his powerful hands, he pulled the chain from the rock.

"How can I thank you, strong Hercules, for saving me?" asked Prometheus.

"Do not thank me," said Hercules. "You gave the gift of fire back to Man. It is my wish to help people who have been kind and good. Come

now, let us go back to the world." The two heroes swam to the boat and sailed home over the
angry sea.

The people of the world were happy to see
Prometheus again. They thanked Hercules for
helping the man who had taken fire from Zeus.
They asked Hercules to stay with them. He said
he would like to stay but that he must go to a
far-off land where there was a king he must help.
He said goodbye and sailed away.

THE LABORS OF HERCULES

AFTER SAILING for seven days and seven nights, Hercules came to the land of a powerful king named Eurystheus. The people of the country had heard of Hercules. They crowded about him and asked why he had come.

"I wish to see the king," said Hercules.

"We will take you to him," the people said.

When they came to the palace, the king came out to meet Hercules. He was a small man with a wrinkled face and a black beard. His eyes were cruel.

"Well, strong Hercules, you have come at

last," said Eurystheus. "I have many things to say to you. Come with me into my palace."

Inside the palace it was cold and dark. Hercules turned to the king and said, "Why have you sent for me?"

The king gave a cruel laugh and said, "The gods have put you in my power, strong Hercules. You will have to do just as I tell you. I am going to make you work very hard."

"Why have the gods done this to me?" asked Hercules with surprise.

"That is not for you to ask," shouted the king. "You must do as you are told."

The earth shook and the sky grew black. Hercules knew that what the king said was true.

Sadly he said, "I shall do as you wish."

For many long years Hercules worked for King Eurystheus. These stories tell of some of the hard labors Hercules had to do for the cruel king.

1

NEAR THE KINGDOM of Eurystheus was the country of Nemea. A lion lived in the mountains of this country. He was so fierce that the people of Nemea were afraid to leave their houses. From their windows, they watched the monster carry off their cows and sheep. Two strong men went out to try to kill the lion. They never came back. Soon even the bravest men hid when they heard the sound of roaring.

King Eurystheus heard about the terrible lion. He called Hercules to him.

"I have heard, strong Hercules, that you are the most powerful man in the world. Tell me, now, is this true?" asked the king.

"Some say that the gods have given me this gift," answered Hercules.

"We shall see. We shall see," said the king.

He told Hercules about the fierce lion of Nemea.

"Are you brave enough to try to kill the lion?" asked the king.

"I should like to help the people of that country," said Hercules. "When shall I go?"

"Go now," said the king. "Bring back the lion's skin to show that you have killed him. This will be your first labor."

The king walked with Hercules to the door of his palace. As he watched Hercules leave, the king said to himself, "You think, strong Hercules, that this will be your first labor. It will be your last. The lion of Nemea will kill you."

With a wicked laugh, the king walked back into his palace.

Hercules walked for five days. He took his mighty bow and arrows with him. The bow was so big that no man on earth but Hercules could shoot an arrow with it. At last he came to the country of Nemea. He looked around, but he could see no one. The cows and sheep moving slowly over the grass were the only signs of life.

He came to a house and called, "Is anyone at home?"

No answer came.

He called again. This time the door opened slowly and he saw the unhappy face of a woman.

"What do you want?" she asked. She seemed very much afraid.

"I have come to help you," said Hercules, "Do not be afraid."

"How can you help us?" she asked. "A terrible lion has come into our country. He has killed most of our sheep and cattle. Now he tries to come into our houses and carry off our children."

"I have heard of this fierce lion," said Hercules. "Where can I find him?"

"You must not look for him," she cried. "He will kill you."

"That may be true," said Hercules, "but I

will not rest until I have tried to save the people of this country."

"You are a brave man," she said. "If you must go, walk until you come to the mountain. It is said that the lion lives at the top in a cold, dark cave."

She put her hand on his arm and said, "May the gods go with you."

Hercules thanked her and watched her lock the door again. Then he set out for the mountain. As he walked, he began to think of a way to kill the lion. He looked at his mighty bow and arrows. Powerful as they were, he wanted something else to help him. He saw a giant tree near by. He said to himself, "This will be just the thing to help me kill the lion. I shall use it as a club."

With his powerful hands, he pulled it from the earth. He put it on his shoulder and walked on.

It was almost night when he came to the mountain. He said to himself, "I shall rest here until morning. Then I shall look for the lion."

He put down his bow and arrows and sat on a rock with his club in his hands. He watched the sun set in the west. The moon came up and sent down its cool light. The stars shone brightly. Hercules could hear the night sounds of the forest. He knew all was well.

All at once a great quiet fell on the forest. Hercules looked up in surprise. By the cold light of the moon, he saw the lion. It walked quietly, like a big cat.

Hercules picked up his mighty bow and arrows. He took careful aim and let the arrow fly. It hit the lion but, to the hero's surprise, it bounced away. He shot another arrow. Again it bounced off the monster.

The lion turned and roared. He saw Hercules and shook his ugly head in anger. Hercules picked up his club. The lion moved slowly toward the hero. Hercules stood his ground. The lion jumped. Hercules, waving his club fiercely, met the monster. Down on the hard ground they fell. Over and over they turned. For a time, it seemed as if the lion would win and that the hero would be killed. But at last Hercules held the lion off, and hit him with his giant club. The lion roared and backed away. Never before had he met a man as strong as Hercules. They stood watching each other quietly. Then Hercules put down his club. He walked to the lion and threw him to the ground. With his powerful hands he killed the fierce monster.

The contest had been long and hard. Hercules lay down to rest, and soon he was asleep.

The next day, Hercules took his knife and skinned the lion. He picked up his bow and arrows and club. With the lion skin over his arm, he left the forest.

When Hercules came to the kingdom of Eurystheus, he went at once to the palace. He put the lion skin over his head. Eurystheus was sitting on a golden chair talking to his friends.

When the king saw Hercules in the lion's skin, he turned white. He was sure a fierce beast had come to kill him. He jumped behind his chair and called to his guards for help.

Hercules gave a mighty laugh and threw the lion's skin to the floor.

"Do not be afraid, King Eurystheus. I shall not hurt you. The lion of Nemea is dead."

Everyone began to laugh. The king was very angry that his friends and his guards had seen

him afraid. He sent them away and turned to Hercules.

"You will be sorry for the trick you have played on me," he said.

KING EURYSTHEUS was very angry with Hercules. Never before had anyone made fun of him. For

many days he would see no one. He sat in his
cold, dark palace thinking of a way to make
Hercules sorry for his trick.

"I must find a labor which Hercules cannot
do," he said to himself.

Many messengers came to the kingdom of
Eurystheus to ask for the help of the mighty hero.
They told of fierce sea monsters and cruel giants

who were killing their people. Again and again they asked King Eurystheus to send Hercules to fight these monsters. Each time the king shook his head. He knew that not one of these monsters was powerful enough to kill mighty Hercules.

One day a messenger came to the palace. He was white and shaking. He fell at the feet of the king.

"What do you want?" asked King Eurystheus.

"You must save us!" cried the messenger.

"Why should I save you?" asked the cruel king.

"A terrible monster has come into our land," the messenger answered.

"There are monsters in every land," said the king.

"There are none like this one," said the messenger.

"Tell me about him," said the king.

"People have always been afraid of giant snakes that live in swamps. Our country has a snake more terrible than any of these."

"How is he more terrible?" asked the king.

The messenger's face turned white. "Not

only is he more fierce and cruel than other snakes, but he has nine heads."

"Nine heads!" cried the king. "It would take a powerful man to kill this monster."

"And not only has he nine heads," said the messenger, "but one of his heads will never die. It is immortal!"

"Immortal!" cried the king. "Do you mean that you cannot kill it?"

"Yes," said the messenger. He shook his head sadly.

The king asked, "What do you call this giant monster of the swamp?"

"We call him the Lernean Hydra," said the messenger.

The king stood up. He knew that he had found a monster so fierce that even strong Hercules could not kill it. He called Hercules to the palace. He told him to go with the messenger into the country of Lernea.

After Hercules had gone, the king smiled a wicked smile. He was sure he would never see the strong hero again.

As Hercules and the messenger left the palace, a young boy came running up to them. He was

Iolaus, the son of Hercules' brother. He cried,
"Where are you going, brave Hercules? Are
you going to fight another fierce monster?"

Hercules put his hand on the boy's shoulder.

"Yes, Iolaus, I am going to do another labor for King Eurystheus."

"Take me with you! Please take me with you! I, too, wish to be a great hero," shouted the boy.

"No," said Hercules with a smile. "You are not yet old enough to go on adventures."

"But I could help," cried Iolaus. "I could drive your chariot."

Hercules looked at the boy's unhappy face. He loved Iolaus and did not want to see him sad.

"Does it mean so much to you, Iolaus? Do you really want to go with me?" asked the hero.

Iolaus pulled his shoulders back. His eyes shone. He held his head high and said, "I should like to be just like you. When I grow up, I, too, want to help the people of the world."

Hercules looked down at the boy. He took his hand and shook it.

"You shall have your wish," he said. "Go get the chariot at once."

Soon Hercules, Iolaus, and the messenger were riding in the chariot on the road to Lernea. As they raced along, the messenger told Hercules about the fierce hydra. He listened as the man told of the nine heads and of the head that would not die. The hero was not afraid.

As they came near Lernea, the messenger began to shake. His face grew pale. He said, "I must leave you now. I am afraid to go any nearer."

Iolaus stopped the chariot. The messenger got out and said, "The fearful swamp is on the far side of that dark forest. You will know that you are near when you come to a place where there are no flowers or trees. Nothing will grow anywhere near the monster's cave."

The messenger began to shake even more. "Go carefully, brave Hercules. May the gods be with you."

He turned and ran away as fast as he could.

Hercules and Iolaus rode to the dark forest. They stepped out of the chariot. Hercules went first. Iolaus walked after him. Soon they came to the other side of the forest. Just ahead, they saw the fearful swamp. It was a terrible sight. For as far as the eye could see there was no living thing. No trees or flowers grew. No birds sang. No fish swam in the yellow water of the near-by river. Not far away they could see the black cave where the hydra lived.

Hercules turned to Iolaus and said, "Stay here. Guard the horses. I shall come back when I have killed the monster."

The hero walked into the fearful swamp. He had the lion's skin over his shoulder. In his hand, he carried his mighty club and his bow and arrows. He looked at the cave where the hydra lived. He took up his giant bow and sent three arrows into the cave.

From the darkness came a hissing sound. Out of the cave came the ugly black hydra. It waved its nine heads as it looked around for something to kill. Hercules hit the nearest head with his club. It fell to the ground. Hercules started to hit another head. To his surprise, he saw that in the place of the first head, two more had grown. Then he knew that he could not kill the hydra alone.

Hercules shouted, "Iolaus, Iolaus!" He did not know if the boy was still with the horses.

"Here I am! Here I am!" cried the boy. He had been afraid when he saw the hydra, but he had not run away.

"I must have fire," shouted Hercules. "Get some as fast as you can."

Iolaus ran to the forest. He set fire to a big tree. He carried the burning sticks to Hercules. He was just in time. The hero's foot was held fast by the hydra.

Hercules called, "I shall hit one of the heads of the hydra. Put a burning stick on the place where the head was. This is the only way we can kill the monster."

Hercules hit one of the heads of the hydra

with his mighty club. Iolaus ran in with the burning stick and put it where the head had been.

The monster fell back with a fearful hissing. Hercules pulled his foot away.

"Well done, brave Iolaus. No new heads will grow in that place!" cried Hercules.

Shoulder to shoulder the two heroes worked, Hercules hitting the monster, Iolaus placing the burning sticks where the heads had been. At last, all the heads were killed. Only the one which could not die was left. Hercules cut it off. Then he carried it in his hands and put it in the ground under a mighty rock. There it would never hurt anyone again.

The next day Hercules and Iolaus set out for home. King Eurystheus was very much surprised to see them. Now he knew that to kill Hercules he would have to trick him. He found a way to do this very soon.

3

FAR TO THE WEST of Greece was a country of which the sailors spoke. Today we call that country Spain. The Greek sailors called it "The

Red Land" because as the sun set, it turned the forests and mountains a beautiful red-gold. Pretty as this country was, the sailors were afraid of it. They had heard that a fierce monster, stronger than any man in the world, lived there. They said that this monster was like other men from the waist down; but from the waist up, he was three men. He had three heads and six arms, and he was as strong as three men together. His name was Geryon. It was said that Geryon had a beautiful herd of cattle which he guarded day and night with the help of his two-headed dog.

In Greece, Eurystheus heard about the fierce monster Geryon and his beautiful herd of cattle. He called Hercules to him.

"Well, strong Hercules, you have done many labors for me and have shown how brave you are. I shall let you go soon, but before you leave my kingdom forever, there is one last labor I want you to do."

"I shall do as you say," said Hercules. "Where must I go this time?"

"Far away," said Eurystheus, "is the land where the sun sets. In this land, is a beautiful herd of cattle. Bring them back to me as soon as you can."

"Is that all you want me to do?" asked Hercules. "That does not seem as hard as the other labors you have given me."

"It will be hard enough," said the king. "They say a man and his two-headed dog guard them. You will have to get them away from him. Go now, and bring them back."

When Hercules had gone, Eurystheus gave a cruel laugh. He said to himself, "I did not tell Hercules that the man who guards the herd of cattle has three heads and six arms and is as strong as three men. He will think that just one man guards the herd."

The king laughed again. "This time strong Hercules will be killed."

Far as Hercules had gone for Eurystheus, he had never been as far as the Red Land. To get there, he had to take a boat to Crete. From there he sailed to Egypt. He walked all the way across North Africa until he came to the strip of water which lies between Africa and Spain. Here at the very end of the world, Hercules stopped. To show he had come so far, he set up two great rocks. The rocks are still there today. The one which is better known is called the Rock of Gibraltar, but the Greeks called both the Pillars of Hercules.

After setting up the rocks, Hercules lay down. He put his bow and arrows and club on the ground. He tried to sleep, but the hot sun beat down on him, and he could get no rest. He was angry, and he took up his bow and shot an arrow at the sun. The sun god, Apollo, riding his chariot across the sky, looked down and saw Hercules shooting arrows at him. The great god laughed. He called down to Hercules, "What, little man? Do you think you can put out the golden light in the sky by shooting arrows at it?"

"I am sorry, Apollo," said Hercules, "but I was angry because the sun was hot, and I could get no rest."

"You are a brave man, Hercules," said Apollo. "Where are you going?"

"I am going to the Red Land to get the cattle of Geryon for King Eurystheus," said Hercules.

"Well, then," said Apollo, "I shall help you to get there. Take this as a gift from me."

The great god put his hand into his cloak and pulled out a beautiful golden cup.

"This cup has magic in it. Use it as you will," he said.

With that, Apollo threw the cup to Hercules and went on his way in his chariot across the sky.

Hercules took the golden cup in his hands and looked at it. He said to himself, "To get to the Red Land, I must sail out onto the great ocean. This cup will be the very thing to get me there."

He took the cup, which was not very big, and set it on the water. The cup began to grow until it became a golden boat. Hercules stepped into it. Soon he was sailing over the bright blue water on his way to the kingdom of Geryon.

Hercules sailed for a long time. He sailed through the small strip of water which is between Africa and Spain into the great ocean. The golden boat flew over the waves.

The old god Oceanus, king of the ocean, saw Hercules going by. He said to himself, "Who is this man who comes into my kingdom without asking me?"

Oceanus shook his long white beard. He

called to the god of the wind, "Shake up the waters! Make them angry! Let us teach this man a lesson he will not forget."

At this, the god of the wind made the ocean roar. He made the sky grow black, and he shook the waters until the waves grew ten feet tall. The golden cup rocked back and forth. Many times it was almost turned over into the dark ocean. Hercules was not afraid. Far off, he could see Oceanus laughing at him. This made him very angry. He took his bow and shot an arrow at the old white-bearded god.

Like Apollo, Oceanus saw that Hercules was a brave man. He called to the god of the wind and said, "It is not every man who is brave enough to shoot an arrow at a god. Let the waters be quiet again so that this man may sail his boat over the ocean."

The wind god did as Oceanus had said, and at once the sun came out and shone on quiet waters. Hercules thanked Oceanus and waved to him as he went sailing by.

It was almost night as Hercules came to the Red Land. As he came near, he could see the cattle of Geryon standing by the shore. The light of the setting sun turned their coats a beautiful red-gold. Hercules sailed nearer. He saw the terrible two-headed dog moving quietly among the herd. Hercules said to himself, "This labor will not be hard. I shall kill the black dog when it is night and then carry away the cattle. If the man who guards the herd tries to stop me, I shall kill him, too."

Little did strong Hercules know what kind of man he was going to have to fight.

Quietly, he landed his boat on the shore. He stepped out and picked up the golden cup. It grew very small. The hero put it in his cloak.

A giant rock stood near the shore. Hercules ran to it and hid in its shadow. From there he could see the beautiful cattle moving over the green grass. He looked for the black dog, but he was nowhere to be seen.

Just then he heard a terrible sound in back of him. He turned and saw the ugly two-headed dog coming at him. The dog jumped, his fierce eyes shining with a yellow light. He locked his teeth on Hercules' arm. With his free hand, Hercules hit the dog with his club. The dog gave a mighty roar and let go. Hercules picked up the beast and, with his powerful hands, shook him until there was no life left in him. Hercules said to himself, "I have killed the terrible two-headed dog. Now it will not be hard to get the cattle."

He stepped out from his hiding place, and began to round up the herd.

To his surprise, the earth began to shake under his feet. The cattle moved away and herded together as if they were afraid. A giant shadow fell across the ground. From out of the forest came Geryon. His three heads shook with anger. His six eyes burned with a cruel light. In each of his six hands, he carried a club. His hairy faces were so ugly that, for the first time in his life, Hercules was afraid.

He said, "Eurystheus did not tell me that so fierce a monster guarded the cattle. He wanted Geryon to kill me."

Hercules ran back to his hiding place by the rock.

The monster roared, "Why are you running, little man? Are you afraid of me? Come out into the open and let me have a look at you."

Hercules said to himself, "I cannot fight with

Geryon. He is not like the other monsters I have killed. He is a man and as strong as three men together. How can I stop him from killing me?''

Geryon came near, waving his six clubs wildly. Hercules picked up an arrow and put it to his mighty bow. He knew he must shoot at once because the sun had almost set. If he missed, there would not be enough light to see the monster.

"I am going to kill you," cried Geryon. Hercules let the arrow fly. It hit Geryon and he fell to the ground. By the last light of day, Hercules saw that the monster was dead.

The next day, Hercules rounded up the cattle again. He said, "It is a long way to the kingdom of Eurystheus. How shall I get the cattle back to him?"

As he was thinking of what to do, he looked up at the sky and saw the sun. He put his hand into his cloak and pulled out the golden cup. He put it on the ground. One by one, the cattle walked into it. Hercules looked up at the sun and thanked Apollo again for the magic gift.

Hercules could not sail back to Greece because he had put the cattle in Apollo's cup. He walked all the way. He went across Spain to Italy and from there overland to Greece.

He had many adventures on the way. Once people tried to steal the cattle. Once they were nearly lost in the mountains, when they were set upon by stinging flies. Hercules had to watch over the herd day and night.

At last he came back to Greece. He went at once to the palace of Eurystheus.

"Are you surprised to see me?" asked Hercules.

Eurystheus was surprised to see Hercules, but he did not show it.

"Have you been to the Red Land?" asked the king.

"Yes, I have been to that far land," answered Hercules.

"Why then did you return without the cattle?" roared the king. "I told you to bring back the herd of Geryon. Were you so afraid of the three-headed monster that you did not try to kill him?"

Hercules laughed. "Your trick did not work. The monster is dead, and I have his cattle with me."

"They must be invisible," said the king, "for I do not see them."

"Look again," laughed Hercules. He pulled out the golden cup, and at once the room was crowded with cattle. They stepped on the chairs. They stepped on the tables. They even stepped on the king.

"Get them out! Get them out!" shouted Eurystheus. Hercules laughed and took the cattle from the room.

Hercules worked for King Eurystheus for many years. After he had done twelve labors for the king, he left that land forever.

Hercules was happy to leave and that his labors were over. He did not think there was anyone in the world more powerful than Geryon.

Little did he know whom he would have to fight in his next adventure!

ADMETUS
❧ AND ❧
ALCESTIS

1

ONE TIME Zeus, king of the gods, became angry with Apollo, the sun god. He sent him down to earth to work for a powerful king named Admetus. Admetus was not like the cruel king Eurystheus. He was a kind man. He let Apollo guard his sheep, which was not a hard labor. As time went by, Apollo grew to like Admetus and they became good friends.

One day Admetus came to the sun god and said, "Today I am both happy and sad."

"How can that be?" asked the god. "How

can you be both happy and sad at the same time?"

"I am happy," said Admetus, "because I have fallen in love with a beautiful princess named Alcestis."

"Why are you sad then?" asked Apollo.

"I am sad," said the king, "because I do not think I can marry this beautiful girl."

"Why not?" asked Apollo. "Any girl would want to marry a king as powerful and good as you are."

"It is very sad," said Admetus, "for I think she does love me. But her father will let no one marry her unless he comes to the palace in a chariot drawn by lions and boars."

"That is bad," said Apollo. "What have you done about it?"

"Everything I could do," said Admetus. "I went to the mountains with my men, and found two lions and two boars. We have fed them every day and taken good care of them. Today we tried to have them pull the chariot."

"Did they pull it well?" asked Apollo.

"They didn't pull it at all," cried Admetus. "They began to fight before they even saw the chariot. They are so fierce that my men cannot get near them. I can never drive them to Alcestis."

"I will help you, Admetus," said the sun god, "because you have been good to me. Go back to your palace and wait for me there."

Admetus went back to his house and waited for Apollo. All at once he heard a sound. He looked up and saw the sun god driving a chariot drawn by two fierce boars and two mighty lions.

"Here you are, Admetus," shouted Apollo. "Here is your chariot. These lions and boars will carry you all the way to your beautiful princess."

Admetus jumped into the chariot. He thanked Apollo. With a mighty roar, the lions and boars set out for the kingdom where Alcestis lived.

When the father of Alcestis saw Admetus coming in a chariot drawn by lions and boars, he called his daughter to him and said, "There is the man you will marry. Go meet him and bring him into our palace."

Alcestis did as she was told. She met Admetus at the gate and walked with him into the palace. That night she was married to him. She was very happy because she had loved him for a long time.

After a few days, Admetus took his beautiful wife back to his own kingdom. There they lived a happy life together. The king was kind, and Alcestis was as good as she was beautiful. Everyone loved them very much.

Then one day the people became very sad. Admetus, who had always been a strong man, grew pale and sick. Men came from far and near to help him, but they left his palace shaking their heads sadly. They knew he was going to die. Apollo came to the palace. When he saw Admetus, he knew the end was near. He went at once to Olympus to ask the gods if they would help.

The gods, too, loved Admetus because he was a good king. They said they would save his life if someone would die in his place. Apollo was very happy when he heard this. He knew many people loved Admetus. It would not be hard to find someone to die for him. He went back to the palace of Admetus and told the king the good news.

Admetus called his bravest men to him. He told them what the gods had said. One by one he asked them if they would die in his place. One by one they shook their heads and left the room.

Admetus said, "They would die for me many

times in battle, but they are afraid to die in
sickness."

He turned to Apollo and said, "Call the people who have worked for me for so long. They
love me, and I am sure one of them will die for
me."

When they came into the room, Admetus told them what the gods had said. He asked them if one of them would die for him. They, too, shook their heads. They loved the king, but they were afraid to die.

At last Admetus said to Apollo, "Call my mother and father. They are old, with not many years left to live. Surely one of them will die for me."

The king's mother and father came into the room. They listened to what the gods had said. They loved their son very much, but they, like the others, were afraid to die. They, too, shook their heads.

All at once the door opened. Beautiful Alcestis ran in. She put her arms about Admetus and said, "I will die for you. I could not go on living, were you to die."

As she spoke, the sky grew black and the walls of the palace shook.

Admetus cried, "No! You must not die!"

Apollo said, "It is too late. The gods have heard Alcestis. Nothing can be done. Alcestis must die."

As the days went by, what the gods had said

came true. Admetus grew strong. Beautiful Alcestis became pale and sick. Powerful Admetus could only watch as Death came nearer and nearer.

Then one dark day, she died. Admetus was so unhappy that he sat in his palace and would not see anyone. He could not sleep or eat. At last, he knew he must bury his beautiful princess. He called all the people of his kingdom to him. They followed him to the place where she was to be buried.

Rain fell on the unhappy crowd. It seemed as if even the sky was crying over the death of the beautiful and loving girl. They put her body in the ground. To show the place where she was buried, they set up a giant stone. Then everyone went home.

2

As ADMETUS came near his palace, he saw a man with a lion skin over his shoulder and a club in his hand. It was Hercules.

Admetus went up to the hero and said, "I am Admetus, king of this country."

Hercules said, "I am on my way to a far land. I have come a long way. May I rest in your palace?"

Admetus did not want to see or talk to anyone. But he knew he must be kind to someone who was new in his country. He said to Hercules, "Come in and stay as long as you wish. What I have is yours."

Admetus was very kind to Hercules. He gave him the best room in his palace and all he wanted to eat and drink. That night they sat at the table for a long time. They talked and heard music. Never once did the king show how unhappy he was.

At last it was time for bed. As Hercules was going to his room, he met one of the women who worked in the palace. Her eyes were red from crying, and she tried to hide her face.

Hercules stopped her and said, "Why are you so sad?"

She answered, "Death has come to the palace. Only this morning The Dark One took away our beautiful princess." She then told Hercules the sad story of brave Alcestis.

For a minute Hercules could say nothing.

Then he walked slowly to his room and sat down to think. He said, "I must help Admetus. He was kind to me. He never told me his unhappy secret. He did not think of himself but did his best to make me happy."

All at once the hero knew what he would do. He would go to the place where Alcestis was buried. There he would stay until Death came to take the body of the beautiful girl. He would fight Death. It would be his greatest adventure! Hercules picked up his club and lion skin. Quietly he left the palace.

It was very dark. No moon shone, and there were no stars to brighten the black sky. Hercules came to the place where Alcestis was buried. He sat down beside the giant stone to watch for Death.

All at once, Hercules felt a cold hand on his shoulder. He picked up his club and turned around. The fight had begun!

In the morning, Admetus heard that Hercules was no longer in the palace. The king went outside to see if he could find the hero. To his surprise, he saw Hercules coming down the road. He was carrying a girl in his arms.

The hero came up the steps of the palace and
pulled back the cloak which hid the face of the
girl. Admetus looked at her and knew at once
it was Alcestis. He put his arms around her and
felt her come to life. For a time, he was so
happy he could say nothing.

At last the good king said, "How did you save my wife from Death?"

Strong Hercules told Admetus of his fierce fight with The Dark One. He told how Death had come stealing to the place where Alcestis was buried. He told how they had wrestled for the life of the beautiful girl. He said that at times it seemed as if Death would win the contest, but at last he was able to take Alcestis from the cold hands of Death.

Admetus and Alcestis looked at each other. They turned to Hercules and Admetus said, "We can never thank you enough for what you have done. Come! Let us tell this great news to everyone."

The three of them walked happily into the palace.

For years Hercules went about the world helping others. The poets of Olympia told of his other battles. On one of his adventures he sailed to a far shore with many other heroes. You will read this story, but first you should meet some of the heroes with whom he sailed on this great adventure.

PERSEUS

I

THE BIRTH
❦ OF ❦
PERSEUS

THERE WAS ONCE a Greek king named Acrisius who was very rich. He had everything he needed to make him happy. He had more palaces than he could count and more herds of sheep and oxen than there are stars in the sky. He loved his riches, but more than all of these he loved his beautiful daughter Danaë. Her happy smile brought sunlight into his life.

One day as he was sitting in the garden, an ugly old man with long white hair and a black coat came up to him.

"What are you doing in my garden?" asked the king in surprise.

"I have come to tell you something that you should know," answered the old man.

"What can someone like you have to say to me?" the king went on. "Who are you?"

The old man said quietly, "I am Dion, the magician."

At this the king stood up because he had heard of Dion.

"What news do you have for me?" cried the king.

"Bad news! Bad news!" And the magician shook his head sadly. "One night, as I looked at the stars, I saw a sign that told of your death!"

At this the king's face grew white. "When am I to die?"

"Your death will come soon if you do not give up part of your riches," said the old man.

"I will give up all my riches to save my life!" cried the king. "You may have my kingdom, my palaces, and everything I own."

The old man shook his head. "To save your life, you must give up the thing you love the most," he said. "You must give up your daughter."

The king cried out in surprise, "My daughter — why must I give up my daughter?"

The old man stood quietly and said, "The stars say that if your daughter lives, she will have a son who will bring about your death."

"But my daughter has no son! How do you know that what the stars are telling is true?" cried the king.

"What is in the stars always comes true," said the old man as he walked away.

The king knew that if he were to live, he must see to it that his daughter had no son. He had her locked in a black dungeon and would not let anyone see her. He had men watch the door night and day.

Danaë was very unhappy locked in her black dungeon. She cried most of the time. She could not see the flowers and trees that she loved so much. She knew why her father had put her in the dungeon, and this made her cry all the more.

"I know that my son would not kill my father," she said over and over again, but there was no one who could hear her.

One day Zeus, the king of all the Greek gods, heard Danaë crying. He looked into the dungeon to see why she was sad. When he saw how beautiful she was, he wanted to marry her. He knew that he must get into her dungeon by magic, because the men would stop anyone who tried to open the door.

One night, when Danaë was crying, she looked up and saw a shower of gold. She did not know it was Zeus, who had used magic to come into the dungeon. She put her hands over her eyes and cried, "What is this golden light? Am I to die?"

"Do not be afraid," said Zeus, "for I have seen you crying and want to help you."

"No one can help me," said the girl. "My father has heard that my son will bring about his death. He has locked me in this black dungeon forever."

"I shall bring sunshine into your dungeon and make it beautiful with all kinds of flowers and big trees if you will marry me," said Zeus.

Danaë looked up and said, "That would make me very happy."

So Zeus and the beautiful girl were married and for many years the dungeon became a happy home.

One day the king was sitting in his garden,

thinking of his daughter. He heard something and when he looked up he saw Dion, the magician. He was very much afraid.

"What is it you want with me this time?" asked the king.

"I have seen more bad news in the stars," answered the old man.

"There can be no more bad news for me," said the king. "My daughter is in a dungeon and no one can see her. She has no son to bring about my death."

The old man said, "There is a new sign in the stars. Your daughter has a son."

"A son!" cried the king, jumping to his feet.

"Zeus and Danaë have been married for many years. Now they have a son called Perseus," the magician went on.

"What am I to do?" cried the king. "Perseus will bring about my death."

The ugly old man shook his head and said, "There is only one thing you can do. You must kill the boy and his mother."

The king looked at the old man. "I shall kill the boy," he said, "but why must I kill my own daughter?"

"She could have more sons," said the magician.

"You are right," answered the king sadly. He sat down, putting his head in his hands.

The old magician went away and the king sat in his garden for a long time. Then he went back into his palace. He called his men together and said, "My daughter and her son, Perseus, must be killed."

"When do you want us to kill them?" asked one of the men.

"Do it as soon as you can," said the king sadly.

The next day the men went to the dungeon and took Danaë and her son to the seashore. There they put them in a box made of wood and sent them out to sea.

For many days, Danaë and her son were in the box. Zeus could not find them. They would have died if a fisherman had not seen the box and saved them. He took the girl and her son to his house. The fisherman's wife gave them something to eat and clean beds in which to sleep.

In the morning they were taken to the king

of a far-off country. This king, too, was rich, and his palace was very beautiful.

When Danaë and Perseus were taken before

him he asked, "What brings you to my country?"

The princess answered, "My father has done this to us. He was told by a magician that my son would bring about his death. To save his life, he tried to kill us both. He sent us to sea in a box, but a fisherman saved us."

The king sat thinking for a time. Then he said, "You may stay at the palace, because you have no home."

Danaë thanked him. She and her son lived in this far-off country for a long time.

The king was kind at first, but after a time he became cruel to them.

II

PERSEUS
🌀 AND 🌀
MEDUSA

As TIME went by, Perseus grew tall and strong. He could jump higher than any other man in the kingdom. He could run faster than the king's best horse. But good as he was at running and jumping, he was even better at using the sword. Every year the king put on games to see who in all the kingdom was best with the sword. Every year Perseus was better than all the others.

At first the king was pleased to see the boy do well in the games. After a time, however, he became afraid that Perseus would take over his kingdom because he was so strong. The king knew that he must find a way to send Perseus out of his country.

One day he called Perseus into the palace and said to him, "You are now a man and have grown tall and strong. It is time for your first adventure."

Perseus smiled because he wanted to go on his first adventure. "Where am I to go?" he asked.

The king answered, "In a far-off country there is a fierce monster called Medusa, whom you must kill."

"What does this monster look like?" asked Perseus.

"I cannot say," said the king. "Everyone who has seen her has been turned to stone."

"By what magic power does this monster turn them to stone?" asked Perseus in surprise.

The king answered, "It is said that her face is so terrible that no one can look on her and live. You may be afraid to try to kill her."

"I am not afraid," said Perseus, pulling out his sword and holding it in his hand. "When am I to go?"

"You must go as soon as you are ready," said the king.

"I shall go now," said Perseus, and he left the palace.

After Perseus had gone, the cruel king smiled and said, "I do not have to be afraid of Perseus any more. Medusa will kill him."

For many days, Perseus walked, looking for Medusa. Everywhere he went, he would ask if anyone knew where the fierce monster could be found, but no one could tell him. He began to think he would never start on his first adventure.

One hot day in a far-off country, he was sitting on a stone, thinking about what he should do next. All at once, he saw a cave which looked like a good place to rest. As he came near the opening of the cave, he looked in and saw three ugly old witches. They were called the Graeae. They wore white dresses and blue cloaks. Their long white hair hung down to the ground. They were singing, and Perseus stopped to hear their song.

"*Witches we are and witches we'll stay,*
Our song we have to sing each day,
About Medusa so ugly and old,
Four things he must have to kill her, we're told.

Helmet and shoes, a shield and a knife,
The man must have who takes her life.
And if anyone should find our eye,
He'll get the helmet and shoes that fly."

As the witches sang, Perseus smiled because he knew that he had found a way to kill Medusa. He watched them for a long time. To his surprise, he saw that the old witches had only one eye for the three of them. This eye they passed from one to the other as they sang. Perseus knew what he must do. Quietly he walked up to the three witches and took the eye from them.

The witches cried out, "Who has taken our eye?"

"I have taken your eye," said Perseus. "I heard your song, and now you must give me the magic helmet and shoes."

"First you must give us back our eye," said the witches.

"Never," said Perseus, "unless you give me the helmet and shoes."

The witches turned their backs to Perseus and talked together quietly. At last one of them went far into the cave and came back carrying the things Perseus had asked for.

"Here are the magic helmet and shoes," she said to him. "Now give us our eye."

Perseus gave the witches back their eye. "Now you must tell me," he said, "how this helmet can help me to kill Medusa."

"Put it on and you will find out," said the first witch.

Perseus put on the helmet and at once no one could see him. He was invisible. He smiled because now he knew the magic power of the helmet. He took off the helmet and said, "Tell me, witches, what magic power do the shoes have? How can they help me on my adventure?"

"Put them on," said the witches, "and you will find out."

When Perseus put on the shoes, all at once

he began to fly. He flew up into the sky and
then came back to the ground, smiling happily.
"I can see how these shoes will help me in my
adventure," he said as he took them off. "Now

tell me where I can find the magic shield and knife."

"We do not know! We do not know!" cried the witches, holding the eye with care. "We have helped you all we can."

Perseus thanked them and left the cave. He walked out into the sunshine, carrying the helmet and shoes. All at once he saw a man and girl standing before him.

"For your adventure, Perseus, you may have the magic knife," said the man.

"And here is the shield," said the girl.

"Thank you very much," said Perseus. "Who are you?"

"I am the god Mercury," said the man, "and this is the goddess Minerva."

"We want to help you kill Medusa because she has turned so many good men into stone," said the goddess. "You will find the monster in a black cave at the top of the hill. Go and do your best."

They handed him the knife and shield and left.

Night was coming as Perseus came to the hill of Medusa. He stopped and put on his helmet and shoes. He made ready his knife and shield. He saw the cave. By the light of the fire that was in the opening of the cave, he saw the men Medusa had turned to stone. He was not afraid but walked on into the cave. All at once, he heard Medusa coming. He knew he must not look at the monster or he, too, would be turned to stone. He used his magic shield as a mirror, and looking into it he saw the fierce face that had killed so many men.

Her eyes were small and black. Her face was wrinkled and old. But it was her hair that made her so ugly, for snakes grew on her head.

Medusa could not see Perseus because he had on his helmet. After a time she sat on the ground and closed her small black eyes. When Perseus knew that Medusa was asleep, he walked quietly up to her. Using his magic knife, he cut off her head.

Perseus walked out of the cave. He saw Minerva and Mercury standing before him.

"I have killed Medusa," he said with a smile.

"You have done well," said Minerva, "but you must take the head with you."

"Why must I take the head with me?" asked Perseus in surprise.

Mercury answered, "You will need Medusa's head on your next adventure."

Perseus went into the cave, picked up the head, and flew away.

PERSEUS

❧ AND ❧

ATLAS

AFTER HE HAD killed Medusa, Perseus flew far away. He carried with him his magic helmet, shield, and knife. He had on his magic shoes. He held the head of Medusa in his hand.

At last he came to the very end of the earth. Here was the kingdom of Atlas. Perseus had heard many stories about Atlas. He was not like other men, for he was taller than the highest hill and stronger than ten of the black bears that walked in the forests near his palace. He was a giant and the biggest man on earth.

Everyone was afraid of him because he was cruel.

Atlas was very rich. He had so many cows and horses that it took him seven days to count them. He had so many sheep that he could not walk about his kingdom without stepping on them. The eggs from his chickens made a hill as high as his palace. But the part of his kingdom which he loved the best was his beautiful garden. In this garden were trees on which grew apples of gold.

For the last ten years, no one had seen the apples. Atlas was so afraid that someone might take them that he did not let any men in his kingdom come near his palace. He put a high stone wall around his garden. The wall had only one door, which was always locked. Atlas would open this door once a day. Then he would walk in his garden and look at the beautiful golden trees.

As Perseus was flying over the kingdom of Atlas, he looked down and saw the golden apples. They looked so beautiful in the sunshine that he wanted to take a better look at them. When he landed, he put on his magic helmet because he wanted to be invisible. As he walked in the garden, he took care not to step on the pretty flowers. He went up to one of the golden trees and looked at it for a long time. He put his hand on one of the apples and said to himself, "I have never seen anything so beautiful in all my life. It is too bad that there is a high wall around this garden. I know that everyone in the kingdom would love to see these apples of gold. I must try to think of a way to help them to get into the garden."

He sat down under one of the golden trees to think. The sun was very hot, so Perseus took off his helmet and lay down on the green grass. He looked at the flowers and heard the sweet song of a bird. Soon he was fast asleep.

As it was time for his walk, the giant unlocked the door in the garden wall and came in to see his beautiful apples. With each step, the ground shook under his feet. The shadow of his head and shoulders turned the hot, sunny day into cold, black night. The giant counted the apples to see if they were all there. Then he turned to go. All at once he saw Perseus sleeping on the ground near one of the trees.

"What are you doing in my garden?" roared Atlas.

Perseus jumped to his feet. He looked up and saw the giant.

"I came into your garden to see your apples and to rest," said Perseus quietly.

"I let no one into my garden," cried the giant.

"I came here only to rest as I have come from a far-off land," said Perseus.

"You must go from my kingdom at once and never come back," Atlas shouted. "Leave here or I shall kill you."

"I have heard of the many men you have killed," said Perseus bravely, "but I am not afraid." He picked up his sword from the grass.

Atlas roared, "Don't you know that I am the biggest and the strongest man on earth?"

"You may be right," said Perseus, "but I will not leave your kingdom until you take down the wall around your garden."

Atlas laughed at Perseus and said, "You are very small to be so brave. What is your name?"

"I am Perseus, son of Zeus," he answered.

Atlas stopped laughing because two days before a magician had told him about a sign he had seen in the stars. The old man had said that a son of Zeus would soon take down the wall around his garden. Now Atlas knew he must kill him. He roared fiercely and walked toward Perseus to step on him with one of his giant feet.

Perseus jumped out of the way. He picked up his shield. He ran to the giant and hit him with his sword.

Atlas laughed. "Your sword cannot hurt me, little Perseus." He pulled the sword from Perseus' hand and cried, "This time I shall kill you!"

Perseus saw a giant arm coming nearer and nearer. He ran to one of the golden apple trees and tried to think what to do. All at once he saw the head of Medusa a few feet away. He ran over and picked it up.

"Where are you, little man?" roared Atlas.

"Here I am, Giant. Look at me, then kill me if you can," called Perseus bravely, holding up the head of Medusa.

Atlas looked down to find Perseus and saw

the head of the monster. Before he could take another step, he began to turn to stone. His hair and beard became forests. His arms and shoulders became cliffs. His bones turned into rocks. He began to grow and grow, until he became the tallest mountain on earth. The many forests on the mountain looked green and beautiful.

Perseus smiled and said to himself, "The cruel giant has become a mountain. Now everyone can come into the garden and see the golden apples."

As he put on his shoes to fly away, Minerva and Mercury came before him.

"You have done well to kill fierce Atlas," said Minerva. "From this day on there will be no wall around the garden." As she said this, Minerva put her hand on the wall, and it fell away.

"Now, brave Perseus, you must fly to a far-away country for your next adventure," said Mercury.

"Where must I go?" asked Perseus.

"Fly over the mountain until you come to

the sea. There you will find your next adventure," said Minerva.

Perseus thanked them and flew away.

PERSEUS

❧ AND ❧

ANDROMEDA

1

Perseus flew over the mountain until he came to the sea. He looked down and saw the white boats on the blue water. He saw fishermen sitting in the sunshine. He saw children playing on the seashore. Perseus said to himself, "How quiet and beautiful the sea looks! What adventure could I find here?"

All at once he heard the sound of someone crying. He looked down and saw a girl standing on a rock. He flew down to see why she was crying. He landed on the rock and, as he came nearer, he saw that she was beautiful. Her hair was as yellow as the sun, and her eyes were as blue as the sea. To his surprise, he saw that she was chained to the rock. He walked over to her and said, "Why are you here? Who has chained you to the rock?"

The girl turned her head away and did not answer. Then Perseus said, "Do not be afraid! I want to help you. Let me use my sword to take the chains from your arms."

The girl shook her head and said, "No, you must not help me! I must stay here."

"Why must you stay here?" asked Perseus.

"Do you see the fishermen in their boats, and the children playing on the seashore?" asked the girl.

"Yes, I see them," answered Perseus.

"I must stay here to save them," said the girl.

"Who would want to hurt them?" asked Perseus.

"In this land there is a fierce sea monster who has killed many people. He has said that he will kill no more if I will give up my life to him," said the girl.

"Why does he want your life?" asked Perseus. "Who are you?"

"I am Andromeda, daughter of the king of this country," answered the girl.

As she said this, Perseus saw two people coming toward him. They were crying, and Perseus knew they must be the mother and father of Andromeda.

"My poor daughter," said the mother. "Is there no way to save her life?"

The king shook his head. "There is no way to save her. There is no man strong enough to kill the powerful sea monster."

Perseus walked up to them and said, "Let me try to kill the sea monster."

"Who are you?" asked the king and his wife.

"I am Perseus," said the young man. "I have not seen the sea monster, but I have killed Medusa who was also fierce and cruel."

"If you could save our daughter from the monster, we would give you anything you wish," said the king.

"There is only one thing I wish," said Perseus.

"Name it and it will be yours," said the king.

"I should like your daughter for my wife," said the young man.

"Very well," said the king. "If you kill the sea monster, you may marry my daughter."

All at once, the king's face grew white. He looked out to sea and saw on top of the water

the giant sea monster. It swam along without
making a sound. It was black and wrinkled and
was longer than ten of the king's boats.

"There is the monster," cried the king. "Do
you still want to try to kill it?"

"I am not afraid," said Perseus as he took
out his sword.

The monster now had seen Andromeda and was swimming toward her as fast as it could. Perseus stood before the princess with his sword in his hand.

"Do not be afraid," he said bravely. "The monster will not hurt you. I will kill him first."

Perseus flew down to the back of the sea monster. He hit it in the shoulder with his sword. The monster roared because, for the first time, it had been hurt. The giant thing shook, trying to get Perseus off its back. Perseus hit the monster again and again with his sword until it went down into the sea.

"The monster is dead. Your daughter has been saved!" said Perseus happily. The young man flew to the rock, and with his magic sword cut the chains that held Andromeda.

The girl's father and mother ran up to them. The king said, "Thank you, Perseus. Come, let us go back to the palace. You shall marry my daughter this very night."

That night the king gave a great feast. Perseus and Andromeda were married. All the people in the kingdom were very happy.

2

JUST AS PERSEUS and the princess were about to leave, a cruel man named Phineus came in the door with some of his men.

"What do you want, Phineus?" asked the king.

"I have come to take Andromeda," Phineus said.

"You cannot take Andromeda. Perseus has married her," the king answered.

"But she was to marry me and be my wife," Phineus said.

"You did not try to save her from the sea monster," said the king. "You were not brave. Perseus saved her and has won her for his wife."

"He shall not have her," cried Phineus. He and his men took out their swords and walked toward Perseus. Perseus took out his sword.

Phineus laughed. "You are one. We are many. What good will your sword do you?"

Perseus saw that his sword would not help him. He picked up Medusa's head and turned Phineus and all his men into stone.

All at once, Perseus saw Minerva and Mercury standing before him.

"You have done well, brave Perseus, on this adventure. Now you must go back to your mother. She is unhappy because the king has been cruel to her," said Mercury.

"Take your sword, shield, shoes, and knife.

"Take also the head of Medusa. They will help you," said Minerva.

Perseus said goodbye to the king and queen. Taking Andromeda with him, he left their land.

After many days, Perseus and Andromeda came to the country of the cruel king. They went at once to look for Perseus' mother. They found her locked in a black dungeon.

Perseus asked, "Why has the king done this to you?"

Danaë said, "The king sent you away to be killed by Medusa. After that, he put me in a dungeon. He did not want me to tell what he had done. Let us leave this country and go back to my father."

Perseus pushed open the door of the dungeon with his sword. When the king and his men tried to stop them, Perseus held up the head of Medusa. At once they were turned to stone.

Perseus said, "We shall leave this kingdom and never come back."

On the way home, Danaë told Perseus the story of his grandfather. She told him why they had been sent from his kingdom. She told him of the sign the magician had seen in the sky.

"Your grandfather was afraid that you, my son, would kill him," she said. "When you were very small, he had us sent out to sea in a box."

"But I would never hurt my grandfather," said Perseus.

"I know that," said his mother. "That is why we are going to his kingdom."

When he saw his daughter, the old king was very happy. He said to himself, "The sign that the magician saw in the stars could not be true. Many years have gone by and Perseus has not tried to kill me. By his face, I can see that he is kind. He will not bring about my death."

The king called all the people in his country to a feast. He told them about the many adventures of Perseus. He asked Perseus to show the people how strong he was. He gave him a big rock. Standing many feet away, he said, "Show the people how far you can throw the rock, Perseus."

The young man picked up the rock and threw it. The rock landed on the king. Perseus ran up to his grandfather and cried, "I did not mean to hit you!"

The old king shook his head and said quietly, "You could not help it. What is in the stars always comes true." He took Perseus' hand and smiled. "My kingdom is yours. Always be a brave and kind man."

After he had said this, the old king died.

Perseus was unhappy for a long time. One day, Minerva came to him and said, "You have been sad long enough. Now you must stop thinking about your grandfather. You must try to be a good king."

Perseus said, "You are right. Here are the knife and shield. My adventures are over for a time. You may use them now."

Minerva took them from him.

"You may also take the head of Medusa," said Perseus. "You can use it to help others."

Minerva took the head of the monster and

said, "From this day on, I shall keep the head of Medusa on my shield," and she left.

For many years Perseus and Andromeda were happy together. They were loved by all the people in their kingdom. Perseus had no more adventures for a long time. Then, one day, he went on the greatest adventure of all. But that is another story.

THESEUS

THESEUS

☷ AS ☷

A BOY

THERE WAS ONCE a powerful king named Pittheus, who lived in Troezen. He had a beautiful daughter called Aethra. From far and near, young men came to ask for her hand in marriage, but she would have none of them. She wanted to marry a king who was both strong and wise. Many of the young men who came to the palace were very strong. They could win any contest in running or jumping, but, sad to say, they could not read or write their names. On the other hand, young men came who were very wise. They would sit all day in the palace, writing beautiful poems to the princess. They had read every book and their handwriting was beautiful to see. Still the princess could not love these pale young men. When she took them riding in the green forests and over the sunny hills, they would bounce up and down and fall off their horses. This made the princess laugh, and she sent these young men home.

No one was surprised when at last Aethra married Aegeus. He was both strong and wise. He could throw the spear better than anyone in Troezen, and he had read many books. Best of all, he was king of the most beautiful city in Greece, which was called Athens. Aethra and Aegeus were happy together for a year or two, but then the king had to go back to Athens. He did not want to leave his beautiful wife, but he knew he must help his people. Before he left, he took Aethra to the top of a high hill which overlooked the palace and said, "Soon we shall have a child, beautiful Aethra. If it is a boy, bring him to this hill when he has grown tall and strong."

"Why must I do that, dear Aegeus?" asked Aethra.

Aegeus took his sword and shoes and buried them in the ground. He placed a giant rock over them. He turned to Aethra and said, "When our child can move this rock, send him to me. Then I shall know he is strong enough to be king of Athens."

Aethra said, "I shall do as you say."

They turned away and walked down the hill.

The next day Aegeus left for Athens. Soon Aethra had her child. She was happy when she found it was a boy. She named him Theseus.

The young boy lived a happy life at Troezen with his mother and grandfather. As the years went by, he grew to be strong and wise. He could run as fast as the wind. He could pull a tall tree from the ground with his powerful arms. He could wrestle with a fierce bear. He would laugh and shout as he rode over the hills with his friends. His voice sounded like the roaring of a young lion.

Theseus liked books as well as games and contests. Many days he would sit reading under one of the trees near the palace. He liked the stories of heroes who had killed fierce monsters and saved the lives of others. He liked the adventures of Hercules best of all. He would read these stories over and over again until he knew them by heart. Then he would lie down on the warm grass and look up at the sky. He would say to himself, "How I wish I were as brave as strong Hercules."

One day, Aethra called Theseus to her. She said, "Well, my son, you are now a young man. You have grown both strong and wise."

"It is true, Mother. The men of the palace have shown me how to be brave in battle. You and Grandfather have tried to teach me to be wise and good. Now it is my wish to go out into the world on brave adventures."

"You shall have your wish, my son. Come with me," Aethra said.

They walked to the top of the high hill which overlooked the palace. They sat down on the giant stone which Aegeus had placed there many years before.

"My son, for a long time I have had a secret which I have not told you. Over the years, you have asked me about your father. I have always told you that he is a good and strong man. Now I am going to tell you who he is.''

Theseus stood up and began to smile. He wanted to know more about his father. He wondered if his father were as wise as the heroes in the books he had read. He wondered if he could be as strong as powerful Hercules.

"Tell me, Mother, tell me who he is!" cried Theseus.

Aethra said, "Your father, my son, is Aegeus, king of Athens.''

She told him the story of the rock, the shoes, and the sword. She told him that he was to go to Athens as soon as he could move the rock. She stood up and said, "See if you are ready to go to your father."

Theseus walked to the rock. He put his powerful hands on the giant stone. On the first try, he pulled it away from its resting place. He looked down and saw the shoes and sword. He picked them up and put them on. His eyes were shining.

"Now," he said, "I am ready to go to my father.''

"Wait, my son," said Aethra. "We must go back to the palace and speak to your grandfather. He will tell you how to get to the city of Athens."

They walked to the palace. Pittheus was waiting for them. He had seen Theseus and Aethra go to the hill. When he saw that Theseus had the sword and shoes, he put his arms about the boy.

"Today I am both happy and sad," said the old man. "I am happy that you have grown to be strong and wise. I am sad because now you must leave us. You are no longer a boy. You are a man and must go on brave adventures."

Theseus put his hand on the old king's arm. "I shall never forget you. If my adventures should take me to the very ends of the earth, I shall always remember my happy life here with you and my mother."

The old man walked away. He did not want Theseus to see that he was crying. After a time, he called Theseus to him and said, "Now I shall show you the way to Athens."

He took his sword and, with the tip, drew a map of Greece in the ground. He put an *x* to show Theseus where Athens was. He put another *x* to show Troezen. He said, "There are two ways to go to Athens. You can go by land or sea."

"I shall go by land," said Theseus, looking at the map. "The trip by sea is far too long. It would take me many days to get to Athens that way."

The old man turned pale. Shaking his head he said, "No, my boy, you must not go by land. The road to Athens is filled with cruel and wicked robbers. They are waiting to kill anyone who comes their way."

Theseus stood looking at the map for a long time. Then he turned to his grandfather and said, "I know what you say is true, but the time has come for me to go on brave adventures. I want to be a hero more than anything in the world. I shall go to Athens by land."

The old man said, "Go by land if you must, Theseus. Find your adventures and meet them bravely. That is the way of a hero."

Theseus picked up his sword and shoes. He said goodbye to his mother and grandfather. From a high hill, they watched him sadly as he set out on his first great adventure.

ADVENTURES
❧ WITH THE ❧
CLUB-BEARER
❧ AND THE ❧
FOOT-WASHER

THE ROAD to Athens was long and rocky. It went up high hills and over roaring rivers. In some places it was sunny, but in others the road became dark and shadowy. In these places, not a sound could be heard. The trees seemed to hide the light of the friendly sun.

As he walked along, Theseus met an old woman. She was picking up sticks for her fire.

When she saw the young man, she jumped and turned pale.

"Why are you afraid, old woman?" asked Theseus kindly.

"Why am I afraid!" she cried. "Don't you know that this road is filled with fierce men? They will kill anyone and take what he has. They are the most cruel robbers in all the world."

"Has no one tried to stop these men?" asked Theseus.

"Last year a very strong man set out to kill them. He was never seen again. If I were you, I would turn around and go back," said the old woman, putting her wrinkled hand on the young man's shoulder.

"I cannot do that," said Theseus. "I must get to Athens."

"Why must you go there?" asked the old woman.

"I am going to see my father, the king," answered Theseus.

"What is your name?" she asked.

"I am Theseus, son of Aegeus," said the young man.

As he said these words, they heard a cruel laugh behind them. They both turned and saw, at the edge of the forest, a man holding a mighty club. He was not like other men. His shoulders and arms were more powerful than those of a giant, but from the waist down he was as small as a child. His legs were as thin as sticks.

"I have been listening to what you said, young man," he hissed. "It is a fine thing to meet the son of a king. Come, shake my hand."

"Don't go near him," cried the old woman as she backed away. "It is the Club-bearer. He will surely kill you."

"Never," said the old man with a hollow laugh. "I am a friendly man. I would not hurt you. I have something to give you. It will help you on your long trip."

If Theseus had been older or wiser, he would not have listened to the words of the Club-bearer. He was too young to know the tricks of cruel men. With a smile, he walked up to the ugly old man and said, "Thank you very much. I should like to have something to help me on my way."

Theseus put out his hand. As he did so, a cruel look came over the face of the Club-bearer. His yellow eyes shone and his ugly black hair stood on end. He took Theseus' arm and held it in his powerful hand. He said, "Now, my young friend, we shall see how far you can go."

The Club-bearer gave a cruel laugh and

waved his giant club fiercely. He tried to hit Theseus. The young man drew away just in time. Pulling out his sword, he said, "You have used your club to hurt the people of this land. I have come to help them. The sword of Aegeus will end your wicked ways." He took his sword and killed the cruel Club-bearer.

The old woman ran up to Theseus. She took his hands and said, "You have been sent from the gods to help us. You are a brave hero."

Theseus shook his head sadly. "No, I am not a hero yet. I was not wise enough to know the tricks of cruel men. Now I know I must be on my guard against them."

"You will be wise in the ways of the world soon enough," said the old woman smiling. "Come, let us go and tell the happy news to the people of this land."

Theseus spent two days with the people of the country. They were very thankful for what he had done. Each day they held games for him. Each night they feasted until the stars grew pale in the sky. They asked him to stay with them. He told them he must go to Athens. When he left, they gave him rich gifts.

Theseus walked for many days without seeing anyone. One hot day he lay down to rest in the shadow of a tall tree. He was almost asleep. All at once, he heard the sound of someone singing. He stood up. Not far away, he saw a tiny old man sitting in a chair on the edge of a cliff. On a table near the old man was a black bowl filled with water. He was sitting there singing a little song to himself.

"One hundred and one have passed my way
And washed my feet both night and day.
And now as I sit here, I wonder who
Is going to be number one hundred and two!"

Just as he finished his song, he saw a young boy coming down the road. He called to him, "Stop right where you are, my fine young boy. You know you can't pass this way without washing my feet."

"Why should I wash your feet?" cried the young boy. "Who are you to tell me what to do?"

"I am the Foot-washer," said the old man with a cruel laugh. "Surely you have heard of me. Surely you know that people must do as I say. If they do not, they are always sorry."

At these words, the boy turned pale. He had heard of the Foot-washer. He had heard stories of wicked things he had done. He ran to the black bowl and started washing the old man's feet.

"Oh, that is fine! That is fine! How good the water feels on my poor old feet," said the Foot-washer. "Now find something with which to dry them. There — behind you — there is something!"

As the boy turned his back, the old man kicked him off the edge of the cliff.

"One hundred and two couldn't get by me!
I'll wait here now for one hundred and three!"

sang the Foot-washer as he sat down in his chair again.

Theseus was very angry. He was sorry that he could not have saved the young boy's life. He stepped out on the road. He walked up to where the old man sat.

"Well, One Hundred and Three, I did not know you would come so soon," laughed the old man.

Theseus did not say a word.

"Come, you must wash my feet before you can pass."

Again Theseus said nothing. He walked to the black bowl and began to wash the old man's feet.

"Oh, that is fine! That is fine! How good the water feels on my poor old feet. Now find something with which to dry them," said the cruel old man.

Theseus turned around. The old man kicked out his foot. Just in time, Theseus stepped aside. The Foot-washer went flying over the cliff. He fell to his death on the rocks below.

Theseus said to himself, "I have killed the Club-bearer and the Foot-washer. Both of them tried to trick me. Each time the trick was shown to me by someone else. Maybe next time I will be wise enough to see the trick myself."

He picked up his sword and club and walked back to the road.

"Now on to Athens," he said.

He knew that his greatest adventures lay ahead of him.

ADVENTURE

❂ OF THE ❂

STRETCHER

Now, as he walked along, Theseus was met by all kinds of people. They had heard news of his brave adventures. They came out of their houses to thank him for helping them. Some showered him with gifts and some called him a great hero. Many people asked him to stay with them, but his answer was always the same. He must get to Athens where his father was waiting for him.

One day, as he was nearing Athens, he came to a part of the road that was very dark. Giant trees hid the blue sky overhead. Black shadows fell on the ground and on the yellow river which ran near by. The only sound he could hear was the roaring of the wind in the trees.

Theseus stopped. He looked around him. He wondered why he had not seen houses or people for so long a time.

He said to himself, "People must be afraid to live in so ugly a place. I wonder if adventure awaits me here!"

Night was falling and Theseus lay down to rest. He was almost asleep when he felt a hand on his shoulder. He jumped up and pulled out his sword. Standing before him was a queer old man. He was tall and very thin. His eyes were small and black. His skin was yellow and wrinkled. He danced up and down as he talked.

"Now, my fine young friend, there is no need for you to sleep on the cold ground tonight. My house is near by. There you will find a bed on which you will rest well."

Theseus looked long and hard at the queer old man. He had heard stories of a wicked robber who lived near Athens. He wondered

if this were the same man. Smiling, he said, "You are very kind. I should like to try your bed."

Together they walked into the dark forest. The queer old man went first, dancing along happily. Theseus walked behind him. Soon they came to an open place in the woods.

"There!" cried the queer old man. "There is my house! It is not a palace, but many a man has passed a quiet night there. Hurry! I want to show you my wonderful bed."

Theseus called to him, "Wait, old man. There is something I wish to tell you before I go to my rest. I am going to Athens. I shall have to be on my way before the sun is up."

"Surely, surely, my friend," said the queer old man dancing up and down. "Many young men have rested here. All of them say they must go by sunup, but after a night on my wonderful bed, they do not wish to go at all."

Theseus smiled. He knew now that this must be the wicked robber about whom he had heard. He did not say a word, but followed him into the dark house. Just as they came in the doorway, the old man took hold of Theseus' arm. He tried to throw him to the floor. This time Theseus was ready for the trick. With his powerful arms, he pushed the old man to the ground and stood over him, sword in hand.

"Did I surprise you, old one?" laughed Theseus. "You did not think I knew you, but I did. You are Procrustes, the Stretcher. You have asked many men to spend the night in your wonderful bed. If they do not fit this bed of yours, you make sure that they do. If they are too long, you cut off their legs. If they are too small, you stretch them until they fit it well. You have given nothing but sadness to the world. Now you must die!"

In no time, the Stretcher met the same end he had given so many others.

Theseus walked away from the dark house. He said to himself, "Again a cruel man has tried to trick me. This time I found out the trick on my own, without the help of another. Maybe now I am becoming wiser in the ways of the world."

Theseus walked to the top of a high hill. From there, he could see the city of Athens. Its towers and palaces shone in the sun. He raced down the hill. Now at last he would find his father.

IV

ADVENTURE ❧ OF ❧ THESEUS ❧ AND ❧ MEDEA

THE PEOPLE of Athens had heard of the brave things Theseus had done. When he came to the gates of the city, they crowded around him. They called him a great hero and said it was good to have a brave and strong man in the city again.

Theseus was surprised at their words. He asked, "Isn't Aegeus, your king, a brave and strong man?"

At these words, a dark look came over the faces of the people.

"He used to be both strong and wise," said one man.

"Yes, he used to be the greatest king in the world," said another.

"What has become of him?" asked Theseus. "Is he sick?"

"No," said a woman. "The wicked witch Medea now lives in the palace. He has fallen under her magic power." Theseus turned pale. He had met Medea and knew how strong her magic was.

"Why does no one drive this wicked woman from Athens?" asked Theseus.

"No one is brave enough. We are all afraid of her magic power," answered the woman.

"I shall go to see your king," said Theseus. "Show me the way."

The people made their way to the palace, carrying Theseus on their shoulders.

Inside the palace, Medea, the wicked witch, heard the sound of the crowd. She went to the window and looked out. She saw the tall hero. She knew, by magic, that it was Theseus, son of

Aegeus. She ran to the old king and hissed in his ear, "Bad news! Bad news! A tall man is coming. He will try to trick you out of your kingdom!"

The old king jumped up and went to the window.

"Is that the man?" he asked, looking at Theseus.

"That is the one," answered the wicked witch.

"We must find a way to get him out of Athens at once," said the old king.

"There is only one sure way," said Medea. "We must kill him!"

"I could not do that," said Aegeus. "I am no longer strong enough."

"I have a way," said Medea. She ran to her room. When she came back, she had a golden cup in her hand.

"Give me a little wine," hissed the witch. "I have put something in the cup to make him sleep forever!"

"Good!" cried the king.

By this time the crowd had come to the gates of the palace. They called Aegeus to come out and meet the brave hero. Aegeus and Medea opened the door of the palace. They stood on the steps and said they were glad to see the young man. Theseus looked for a long time into his father's eyes, but his father did not know him. Sadly the tall hero walked into the palace with the king and the wicked witch.

That night, Aegeus gave a great feast for Theseus. The table was ten feet long. On it were cups and bowls filled with all kinds of food and wine. Theseus kept watching his father, hoping he would remember him. The old king never once looked his way.

At last, Medea came out carrying the golden cup.

"Do not drink the wine that is on the table, young man," she said. "We have saved the best wine in all the kingdom for you. We will give it to you in our best cup."

She handed the golden cup to Theseus. She smiled at him. Something in her wicked face told Theseus it was a trick. He looked at his father. Slowly he pulled out his sword. He laid it on the table near the king. At once Aegeus jumped to his feet.

"Theseus! My son!" he shouted. With the

sword, the old king sent the golden cup flying
to the floor. The old man threw his arms around
the hero's neck.

"I have waited for you a long time, my son,"
said Aegeus.

"Why didn't you know me when I first came?" asked Theseus.

"I have been in the power of Medea, the wicked witch. Now at last you have saved me!" said the king.

Theseus looked around. Medea was not in the room. The tall hero ran down the palace steps. At the gate he called the guards and asked if they had seen her. They said that she had run away into the night.

From that day on, Medea was never again seen in the city of Athens.

V

THESEUS

❧ AND THE ❧

MINOTAUR

FOR MANY DAYS Theseus and his father were happy together. One day they were sitting in a garden near the palace when a woman came before them. She was crying, and she threw herself at the feet of the old king.

"O King Aegeus," she cried, "you must save my child!"

"I will do what I can," he said kindly. "How can I help you?"

"Do not send my son to Crete," she cried.

"He is my only child. His father is dead, and he is all I have in the world."

"Why must he go to Crete?" asked Theseus, helping the poor woman to her feet.

Aegeus shook his head sadly. Then he told his son the story of the terrible Minotaur of Crete.

"As you know, my son," he began, "to the south of Greece lies the island of Crete. The king of this land is a cruel man named Minos. He is far more powerful than we are. Every year he makes us send seven boys and seven girls to his kingdom."

"What does he do with these young people?" asked Theseus.

"We are not sure," answered his father, "for we never see them again. We do know that he keeps the Minotaur near his palace. Some people think that the children of Athens are given to this fierce monster!"

"What kind of monster is the Minotaur?" asked Theseus.

"It is almost too terrible to tell about," answered the king. "I have heard that it has the body of a man and the head of a bull.''

The woman had been listening to the story. When Aegeus had stopped talking, she threw herself at his feet again.

''You must not send my son to be killed by this terrible monster,'' she cried.

Theseus stood up. ''Do not cry any more,'' he said. He put his hand on the shoulder of the poor woman. ''I will go to Crete in the place of your son.''

The king jumped to his feet. He put his hand on Theseus' arm. ''No, my boy! You must not go!'' cried the old king. ''The people of Athens need you here. Some day you will be their king.''

''I will be a better king to the people of Athens if I free them from the power of King Minos. I will sail to Crete tomorrow,'' said Theseus.

Aegeus knew there was nothing he could do to stop the hero. He turned to the woman and said, ''Tell the people that Theseus will go to Crete in the place of your son.''

The woman threw her arms around the powerful shoulders of Theseus. She thanked him again and again. At last, she ran from the garden.

The next day, before the sun was up, Theseus made ready for his trip to Crete. Once again he put on his father's sword. He picked up his shield and knife. Then he walked down to the place where the Greek ship was waiting.

Aegeus had come to see the ship sail. He turned to Theseus and said, "Look at the ship, my son. I have had the men put up a black sail. If you kill the Minotaur, put up a white one in its place. I shall watch for you every day from the high cliff by the sea. If I see the white sail coming, it will be a sign to me that you have killed the monster. If I see the black sail, I shall know that you are dead."

"I shall remember what you have said," answered Theseus. "A white sail means we have won. A black sail means we have lost."

Theseus stepped onto the ship. From the shore, his father cried, "May the gods go with you!"

For many days the ship with the black sail flew over the bright blue waves. At last it came to the island of Crete. Here it was met by a great crowd of people. They had come to see the new boys and girls from Athens. They were pleased to see tall Theseus, who towered above the others.

In the crowd was Ariadne, beautiful daughter of king Minos. Never before had she seen a man like Theseus. She fell in love with him at once. Her eyes followed him as he made his way slowly to the palace.

Minos, the cruel king, was waiting for them. He had been told that Theseus, son of Aegeus, had come. He knew the hero at once. He looked at him and said, "Do not think that you will be saved from death because you are the son of a king. You, too, will be given to the Minotaur."

"I have not come to be saved from death," answered Theseus. "I have come to save others. I am going to kill the Minotaur."

Minos gave a great laugh. "That will be hard to do without a sword," he said. "You will not be so brave when you face the monster unarmed."

Minos called for the guards. They took Theseus and his friends to a dark dungeon. They

took away their swords and locked the door.

Late that night, Theseus heard footsteps outside the dungeon. He jumped up just in time to see the door opening slowly. There, by the light of the moon, he saw beautiful Ariadne. In her hand was a sword and a spool of thread.

"Come with me," she said quietly. "Do not make a sound. The guards are everywhere."

He followed her out into the bright moonlight.

"Where are we going?" he asked.

"I am taking you to the labyrinth," she answered.

"What is the labyrinth?" asked Theseus in surprise.

"It is the place where the Minotaur lives. It was made many years ago by a friend of my father's. In the labyrinth there are more halls and doors than you could count. Only one hall leads to the Minotaur."

"How shall I know which hall that is?" asked the hero.

"Always turn to the right," said the girl. "That is the secret of the labyrinth."

"How must I get out?" asked Theseus.

She gave him the golden thread. "This will help you," she said. "As you go into the labyrinth, unwind the thread. After you have killed the Minotaur, follow it back to me."

She handed him the sword. "Hurry!" she said. "It is getting late."

Theseus went into the dark labyrinth. Everywhere he looked there were doors and halls. He remembered Ariadne's words and always turned to the right. Soon he could hear the roaring of the Minotaur. With each door he opened, the sound grew louder. At last he stood outside the monster's room. He threw open the last door and ran in. With his powerful sword, he ended the life of the terrible Minotaur. He looked at the ugly monster and said, "You will no longer kill the young men and women of Athens." He picked up his sword and walked out of the room. The golden thread shone in the darkness. Theseus followed it until he was again at Ariadne's side.

"I am thankful you are safe," she cried. "Come, we must hurry. It is nearly morning and soon the guards will be here."

They ran to the dungeon and unlocked the

door. Theseus called to his friends and told them what he had done. Soon they were all racing to the Greek ship by the shore. As soon as they had set sail, they saw the palace guards running down the hill. They knew they must hurry if they were to get away from Crete.

Soon Theseus and his friends and Ariadne were sailing over the shining water. Behind them, they could see the ships of King Minos. For a time, it seemed as if the men of Crete would overtake them. But as the day went on, the Greek ship pulled far ahead, and at last they were alone on the wide sea.

That night they stopped at the island of Naxos. It was not long before they were asleep, for the day had been long and hard. As the sun came up, one of the boys cried out, "A sail! A sail! Hurry! We must be off! The men from Crete are here!"

Everyone flew to the ship. They put out to sea as fast as they could. Again they had to race with the fast ships of Crete. Again they won the contest.

Not until the race was over did they find

that Ariadne had been left behind on the island of Naxos.

"We must go back for her at once," cried Theseus. "She saved our lives."

"No! No, we cannot do that!" cried the others. "The men of Crete would surely kill us!"

"You are right," said Theseus sadly. "There is nothing we can do. May the gods watch over her!"

Soon they were near Athens. In their hurry, they had forgotten the words of Aegeus. They had not taken down the black sail.

For many days, Aegeus had been sitting on the high cliff watching for the Greek ship. When at last he saw it, he groaned. He knew that the black sail was a sign of Theseus' death. He said to himself, "I no longer wish to live if you are dead, my son!" With these words, he jumped into the sea. To this day, the body of water into which he jumped is called the Aegean Sea.

When he came into Athens, Theseus did not know that his father was dead. He ran to the palace to give Aegeus the good news about the Minotaur. When he heard the story of his father's sad end, he was very unhappy. He went into the palace and would see no one. He would not eat or drink.

At last, the people of the city came to him. They cried out, "We need you! Athens must have a king!"

Theseus knew that what they said was true. He tried to put aside his sadness for the people of the city. From that day on he was known as a strong and wise king.

ORPHEUS

۞ THE ۞ UNDERWORLD

Many times the Greeks told of a dark kingdom called Hades. They said people went to this place when they died. No one was sure where Hades was. Some said it was at the edge of the world. Others said it was under the very ground upon which men walked. That is why some people called it the Underworld.

The kingdom of Hades had two parts — one beautiful, one ugly. The beautiful part was filled with sunlight and happiness. Here lived those who had been good on earth. The other part was dark and sad. Those who had been wicked lived here.

When a man died, Mercury came to take
him to the Underworld. He led him down a
dark road until they came to a great river. This
river was called the Styx. Here Charon, an old
boatman, was waiting. If the dead man had a
penny in his mouth, Charon would take him
across the river in his boat. He would not take
him if the dead man's friends had forgotten
the money.

Once across the river, they came to a dark

palace. Here lived Pluto, King of the Underworld, and his beautiful wife, Proserpina.
Outside the gate sat Cerberus, a fierce three-
headed dog with a hissing snake for a tail. He
would let everyone pass into the palace. He
would let no one out.

Inside the palace, it was cold and dark. The
king and queen sat quietly on black chairs.
Their pale faces were sad. They were so still
that they looked as if they were made of stone.

Into this room, Mercury would lead the man
who had died. Pluto would ask Mercury if the
man with him had led a good life. If the mes-
senger-god said yes, the king sent the man to
the beautiful part of Hades. If Mercury said
no, Pluto gave the man some terrible labor.

Pluto had given terrible labors to many
wicked men. One man had to roll a giant rock
up a hill. Just as he came to the top, a magic
power pushed the rock away from him. Down
it would go, and the man would have to try
once more. He would push the rock to the
top again and again. Each time it would roll
back.

Tantalus had been a cruel man on earth.

In Hades, he had to stand in water which came up to his shoulders. But when he tried to take a drink, the water would run away. He was always thirsty. Over his head grew apples and oranges. But when he put his hand out for them, they would fly away. He was always hungry.

Pluto had also given hard labors to cruel women. Three sisters who had been wicked and mean had to carry water from a well in a sieve.

The people of the world were afraid of Hades. They did not want to go to this dark place until their time had come. Once in a long time a mighty hero had to go to the Underworld. The next story tells of one of these heroes.

II

ORPHEUS
🌀 GOES TO THE 🌀
UNDERWORLD

IN ALL OF Greece there was no better singer than Orpheus. When he sang and played his lyre, people would stop their work and hurry to his side. Animals of the forest would come near. Fierce monsters would sit quietly at his feet. Even tall trees would bend their heads to hear his song.

Orpheus went from place to place singing his songs of love and battle. One day he saw a beautiful girl in the crowd. He fell in love with her at once. He stopped playing and walked over to her.

"What is your name?" he asked.

"I am called Eurydice," she said quietly.

"I shall sing my next song for you," said Orpheus.

He picked up his lyre and sang a beautiful song. When Eurydice heard the song, she fell in love with the singer.

For many days, Orpheus stayed in this place. No longer did he wish to go about the world singing. He wanted only to please Eurydice. Every day he sang her a new song of love.

Then one fine day, Orpheus and Eurydice were married. All their friends came to wish them happiness. There was a great feast. There was dancing and singing. Everyone was very happy until an old man stepped out of the crowd and said, "Stop the dancing! Stop the singing! There is something I must say!"

"What is it, old man?" asked Orpheus.

"I have seen a bad sign in the sky. There is sadness ahead for you and your wife," he answered.

"How can there be sadness for us?" laughed

Orpheus. "We love each other too much to be unhappy."

"We shall see. We shall see," said the old man as he walked quietly away.

After the old man had gone, a dark shadow fell on the feast. Soon everyone went home.

The next day, Orpheus and Eurydice took a walk beside the river. As they came near a field, Eurydice saw some beautiful red flowers. She ran to pick them. All at once, she fell. Orpheus raced to her side. Just as he came near, he saw a snake moving away in the grass.

"My foot! My foot!" cried Eurydice. "Something has hurt my foot!"

Orpheus picked her up in his powerful arms. He ran as fast as he could. He wanted to get to the river to wash her foot. As soon as he put her down on the ground, he knew she was dead.

For a long time after this, Orpheus went about the world singing and playing his lyre. No more did he sing of love and battle. His songs now told of the great sadness he felt in his heart. Each song asked how he might get Eurydice back. He sang to the people of the world. He sang to the gods on Mount Olympus. No one could help him.

At last, Orpheus knew he must go to Hades. He went at once to the black cave which led to the Underworld. Down, down the dark road he went, singing his song of sadness all the way. Soon he was at the River Styx. Here stood the fierce old boatman. He had heard Orpheus coming. He, too, had felt the magic power of the hero's song. He took him across the river without a word.

On into the kingdom of Hades walked Orpheus. At the sound of his singing, Tantalus forgot how hungry and thirsty he was. The man pushing the rock stopped his hard labor. The three sisters put their sieves on the ground and listened to the beautiful music. Orpheus walked on. He passed the cruel three-headed dog and went into the palace of Pluto. Here he saw the king and queen. He fell on his knees before them. Looking up, he said, "I have come to ask you to give me back my beautiful Eurydice. I cannot live without her."

The king and queen had heard the young hero's song. Their hearts had been moved by its sadness. Pluto said, "No one has ever left Hades before. We will let Eurydice go because of your beautiful singing."

"You are very kind, Pluto," said Orpheus. "Where shall I look for her?"

"Do not look for her," said the king. "Go back the way you have come. She will follow you. Do not look back at her until you can see the light of the sun. If you once turn, she will be lost forever. Now, go! Remember my words!"

Orpheus started the long trip back. Out of the palace he went. He passed the three-headed dog. He went over the river. Soon he was on the dark road which led up to the world. As he walked, he listened for footsteps behind him. He heard nothing. He began to wonder if Pluto had played some terrible trick on him. He walked on. Still he could hear nothing. Orpheus could stand it no longer. Just as he reached the end of the road, he turned around.

"Eurydice!" he called.

There before him, he saw a gray shadow. It was his beautiful wife.

"Orpheus!" she cried. "You should not have

turned so soon! We were almost free! Goodbye! Goodbye!"

With a sad smile, she went back to the Underworld. Orpheus followed her, but this time

no one would listen to his song. He knew she was lost forever.

After a time, Orpheus went back to the world. Never again did he sing a song of love!

MELEAGER

THE

🟤 THREE 🟤

FATES

Many Greek poems tell about three old women named the Fates. It was said that they sat at a giant spinning wheel. On the wheel there was a thread for each man on earth. The Fates would add a new thread when a man was born. They would cut the thread when he died.

One winter day, the queen of a powerful country was sitting in her chair. She was rocking her newborn baby, Meleager, in her arms. She was very happy as she looked down at his beautiful face. Outside, the wind was roaring in the trees. Inside, the room was warm and still. The dancing light of the fire threw shadows upon the wall. All at once, the queen looked up. She saw, to her surprise, that the shadows looked like three old women. She moved nearer and saw before her the Three Fates. They were talking together quietly.

"Where is the new thread?" asked one.

"Here it is! I have it!" said another.

"How fine it is! How bright!" said the third, holding the thread in her wrinkled hand.

"Whose thread is it?" asked the first.

"It is Meleager's," said the next.

"Will he have a long life?" asked the third.

"Not long. You will soon cut it," said the first.

"How long?" asked the second.

"Do you see the wood that is even now burning in the fireplace?" asked the first.

"We see it! We see it!" cried the other two.

"When the wood is gone, Meleager will die!" said the first.

The queen turned pale. She looked down at her sleeping child. When she looked at the wall again, she could see nothing but the shadows of dancing leaves. The Fates had gone.

She ran from the room. In no time she was back, carrying a great bowl of water. She threw the water on the fire. Carefully, she picked up the wood and put it in a large black box. She locked the box and hid it in a secret room of the palace. She ran back to her baby. Holding him in her arms, she said, "Now you will be safe. No one will know our secret. The wood is hidden. Your life will go on for many years."

No one found the wood, and Meleager grew to be a fine young man.

The country in which Meleager lived was very lovely. The fields were bright with flowers. The forests were cool and green. The deep rivers sang as they raced on their way to the sea.

Each year Meleager's father, the king, held a great feast on the top of a high hill to thank the gods for his happy land. First he thanked Apollo for his gift of the sun. Then he thanked Vulcan for the warm light of fire. He thanked Neptune for his gift, the shining sea. Last of all, he thanked Zeus, king of the gods, for all the wonderful things he had given Man.

After the feast was over, the king walked home. He looked at the bright stars in the sky. Suddenly, a black shadow hid the light of the moon. The king fell to his knees. He remembered that he had forgotten to thank Diana. All at once the night became as bright as day. The goddess stood before him. Her face was dark with anger.

"O Goddess of the Moon!" cried the king. "I am sorry that I forgot to thank you for your great gift. I thank you now with all my heart!"

"Too late. Too late," said the goddess. "The feast is over, and the people have gone home. Tell them for me that in two days I will send a sign of my anger. They will not forget me again!"

With these words, the goddess walked away. The night became black once more.

On the morning of the second day, messengers came running to the palace. They ran to the room where Meleager and the king were sitting. Their faces were pale, and their knees were shaking. One of them cried, "There is a terrible monster in the forest! It is a boar, but bigger than any other boar in the world!

Already it has killed seven people!"

The king shook his head sadly and said, "This is the sign that Diana said she would send."

For many days the boar ran in the forest and over the fields. It killed everything that stood in its way. At last, the king called Meleager to him. He said, "My son, I had hoped that Diana would forget her anger and send the boar away. Today it has killed ten more people. We must find a way to stop the fierce monster."

Meleager answered, "Let me go into the forest and kill the terrible boar."

The king said, "I know you are brave, but you could not kill the boar by yourself. The boar was sent by the gods. It is more powerful than other animals."

"There is only one thing to do," said Meleager. "I shall send for all the bravest heroes in Greece. Together we shall battle the fierce boar."

"Good!" said the king. "We shall send the messengers at once."

That very day, messengers were sent north, east, south, and west. They carried the news of the fierce monster to every part of Greece. Soon all the bravest young men in the land were on their way to help Meleager and his father.

BATTLE
❂ WITH THE ❂
WILD BOAR

Meleager was glad that so many brave men had come. That night he gave a great feast. As the young men sat laughing and talking, the door opened. A beautiful girl stepped into the room. Her hair was the color of gold, and her skin was white as snow. In her hand she carried a bow and arrows. The men knew at once it was Atalanta.

Atalanta was the daughter of a near-by king. As a child, she had spent her time in the woods. She knew the songs of all the birds and the ways of all the animals. She loved to run with the wind and to swim in the cool waters of the deep rivers. As she grew older, she could run faster than any man. She could shoot her arrows farther than the eye could see.

As the years went by, Atalanta became very beautiful. Many men wished to marry her, but she would have nothing to do with them. She wanted to be free. Now she had come to Meleager's palace to hunt the cruel boar.

At sunup the next day, the hunting party met in front of the palace. Their spears and arrows shone in the sun. They laughed and talked together as the hunting dogs barked happily.

Then Meleager took up his shield and spear. Atalanta made ready her arrows. The whole party moved quietly toward the forest.

They walked deep into the woods. Suddenly they heard a terrible sound. The boar came roaring out of the dark forest. Its giant body was wrinkled and ugly. Its tiny eyes burned with anger.

The men stood their ground. One by one the heroes shot their arrows. One by one the arrows missed the body of the fierce monster. The boar raced toward the heroes. The men flew from him like leaves before the wind. They climbed trees. They hid behind rocks. One man even jumped into the river. Only Meleager and Atalanta stayed to face the cruel monster. Atalanta put an arrow to her bow. She let the arrow fly. Her aim was true, and the arrow went deep into the side of the terrible boar. The monster roared with anger. It tried to run, but it was badly hurt. Meleager took his spear and ended the life of the powerful boar.

The men left their hiding places. They crowded around Meleager and called him a mighty hero. One man took his knife and skinned the boar. He gave the skin as a prize to Meleager. Meleager shook his head and said, "The prize is not mine. It belongs to Atalanta. She was the first to hurt the boar." He turned to Atalanta and gave her the boar's skin.

The men did not like the words of Meleager. They did not like to think that a woman had been brave when they had been afraid.

Meleager's uncles were in the hunting party.

They said to each other, "This woman must not have the prize. Let us take it from her." They moved toward Atalanta and took the skin from her.

Meleager was very angry. He cried out, "You shall not have the prize! Give it to me!"

His uncles gave a cruel laugh and said, "Come and get it then!"

Meleager walked to the place where the two men were standing. As he came toward them, they drew their swords. Soon a fierce fight had begun. Meleager's uncles were as powerful as they were wicked. It seemed as if they would surely win the fight, but Meleager battled like a young lion. Strong as his uncles were, they were not as strong as he. In the end, the two cruel men lay dead on the ground.

Back at the palace, the king and queen had heard that Meleager had killed the boar. They had not been told of the death of the queen's two brothers. The queen went to the top of a high hill to thank the gods for their help in saving the kingdom. As she came down, she saw the bodies of her two brothers being carried on the shoulders of the palace guards.

She put her hands to her face and cried out, "Who has done this terrible thing?"

"Your son, Meleager, has killed them," said the guards sadly.

The queen ran to her room as fast as she could. She sat down to think. She said to herself, "Meleager has done a terrible thing. When I saved his life as a baby, I did not think he would grow up to kill others."

The queen went to the secret room in the palace where she had hidden the black box. She took the box back to her room and opened it. She took the wood out and put it in the fireplace. Soon it was burning brightly.

Meleager and Atalanta were walking slowly back to the palace. They were happy together. Suddenly Meleager fell to the ground. He cried out, "I feel as if a great fire is burning in my heart!"

Atalanta ran to the river. She carried back cold water and put it on Meleager's face, but nothing could help him. The hero died.

It was not long before Meleager's unhappy mother died also. The king was very sad, but never again did he forget to thank all the gods.

THE ARGONAUTS

I

JASON
❦ SETS ❦
SAIL

LONG BEFORE the stories you have read in this book took place, there lived in Greece a young man named Jason. As a baby, he had been put in the care of a wise old centaur. The centaur was half man, half horse. From his head to his waist, he had the body of a man. From his waist to his feet, he had the body of a horse.

The wise old centaur held a school for boys in the woods. Many of the kings of Greece sent their sons to him because he was a great teacher.

The centaur wanted to teach the boys to be brave and strong. He would not let them sleep on beds. He made them sleep outside on the hard ground. He made the boys swim in the cold river even in winter. He showed them how to use the spear, the sword, and the bow. He showed them how to run, to jump, and to race their horses.

The old man also wanted to teach the boys to think. Each day he showed them how to read and write. He had them make poetry and play the lyre.

The old centaur loved all the boys in his school, but he loved Jason best of all. He had watched him grow from a tiny baby to a strong and wise young man.

Jason had heard the story of a magic sheep whose wool had been made of gold. When the sheep had died, the king of a far-off land had cut off its skin. He had hidden it in a secret place. People called the wool the Golden Fleece.

Many brave men had sailed to the far-off land to get the Golden Fleece. They had not come back. It was said a fierce dragon guarded the wool both day and night.

Jason wanted his first adventure to be a great

one. He said to himself, "I shall sail to that far-off land. I shall bring back the Golden Fleece." He sent for all the brave heroes who lived in Greece at that time. They were glad to come. They, too, wanted to go on a great adventure.

First came brave Perseus, who had killed the fierce Medusa. He was followed by strong Hercules, carrying his mighty club. Next came tall Theseus, holding his powerful sword. Then Admetus came, driving his golden chariot. Last came Meleager and Orpheus, both brave heroes.

As soon as the heroes had met, Jason took them to the shore. He wanted them to see the ship which had been built for the trip. The ship was the biggest ever to sail the seas. It was longer than five ships together. It was as fast as the wind.

The ship was called the *Argo* after the man who had built it. The heroes said that they would call themselves the Argonauts.

The next day, Jason and the heroes started on their long trip. Soon the Argonauts were sailing over the wide and shining sea.

The men had many adventures on the way to the land of the Golden Fleece. Some of these adventures the heroes would never forget.

One evening, the Argonauts had stopped to rest on a small island. Suddenly they heard a terrible sound overhead. They looked up and saw giant birds flying over them. Jason picked up his bow and shot an arrow at the bird nearest to him. To his surprise, the arrow fell away. The birds came nearer with angry cries. They did not seem to be afraid of the swords and spears which the heroes waved at them. Jason cried out, "Run! Run for your lives! The birds are made of bronze. Their feathers are arrows!"

The men turned and ran toward their ship. The birds began to shoot their feathers of bronze. The men put their shields over their heads to keep off the arrows which were now falling like rain. They jumped on their ship and sailed away from the terrible birds as fast as they could.

THE LAND ❀ OF THE ❀ GOLDEN FLEECE

ONE DAY, as the Argonauts were sailing along, they saw ahead of them two rocky islands in the sea. As the men came nearer, they were surprised to see the islands move, first together, then apart.

One of the men cried out, "Those are the Clashing Islands! We must sail between them to find the land of the Golden Fleece!"

"How can we sail between them?" cried another. "We shall surely be killed!"

Jason stood up and said, "There is a way we can sail safely by them. I will show you."

The hero took a small white bird. He let it fly away toward the islands. As it flew between them, giant rocks came together with a roaring sound. The little bird was unhurt. It had flown safely between the rocks having lost only its tail feathers. As the islands moved apart, the heroes sailed toward them. Nearer and nearer they went. As soon as the opening was big enough, the men began to sail the ship between the cruel rocks. Slowly, slowly, the great ship moved over the dark and angry waters.

"Hurry!" cried Jason. "The islands are beginning to close!"

The ship sailed on. The shadow of the rocks came near. Just as the islands were about to clash, the ship sailed out into the open sea. The heroes held on as giant waves rocked the ship. They laughed and shouted happily, knowing that they were safe.

It was not long after this that the Argonauts came to the land of the Golden Fleece. They went at once to the palace of the king. They asked if they might have the Fleece to take back to Greece.

The king of the land was a cruel and wicked man. He wanted to keep the Fleece for himself. He said to the heroes, "Many men have wished to take the Fleece. They were not brave enough. I am willing to give it to any man who can do two hard labors for me."

Jason jumped to his feet and cried out, "I will do the labors. What are they?"

The king said, "I have two fierce bulls with feet of bronze. If you can plow a field with these powerful bulls, you will have done the first labor."

"What is the second labor?" asked Jason.

"In my hand I hold the teeth of a cruel dragon," said the king. "After you have plowed the field, you must plant these teeth. From them will grow fifty armed men. You must fight these men. If you can do these two labors, the Fleece will be yours."

The other heroes cried out, "The labors are too hard! No one man could fight fifty armed men and live!"

Jason said, "The labors are hard, but I shall try. I shall come to the palace tomorrow."

The heroes stood up and went back to the ship. They were sad, for they were sure that Jason would be killed the next day.

That night, when everything was still, Jason saw a dark shadow moving near the ship. He picked up his sword and jumped to the shore. To his surprise he saw a girl coming toward him. It was Medea, the daughter of the wicked king. At this time, Medea was a young girl, just learning to use her magic powers. As she grew older, she became as wicked as her father and tried to kill Theseus.

Jason looked at the girl and asked, "Why have you come to the ship?"

"I have come to help you," she said.

"How can you help me?" asked the young man.

"I have magic power," said the girl.

Jason and Medea stood talking for a long time. She gave him a magic charm and a small stone, both of which she said would help him in his labors. As Medea was leaving, Jason turned to her and asked, "Why are you helping me?"

The girl answered, "You are young and strong. I do not wish to see you killed."

The next day, Jason and all the heroes went to the palace. The king was waiting for them. He took them to the place where the bulls with the bronze feet were kept. Jason had the magic charm in his hand. He walked over to the fierce bulls. The animals shook their heads and gave an angry roar, but they did as Jason wished. In no time, they were plowing the field.

The Argonauts, watching Jason, shouted happily. The wicked king's face grew dark. He said to himself, "I did not think that Jason could do this first labor. Still he will not take the Fleece. The armed men will kill him."

When the field was plowed, Jason took the dragon's teeth and planted them in the earth. Out of the ground jumped fifty armed men. They started to battle Jason with their many swords and spears. The hero knew he would be killed if he could not stop their fighting.

He backed away. He took out the stone which Medea had given him and threw it into the field. At once the armed men turned away from Jason and started to fight each other. Soon every one of them was dead.

The king was too surprised to say a word. He walked angrily back to his palace. He called his guards to him and said, "Jason must have had a magic charm to help him do the two labors. Go at once and find out who gave him the magic power."

One of the guards said, "I know who helped Jason. It was your daughter, Medea. I saw her talking to him late last night."

The king cried, "Get your swords and spears! We shall go and kill these men who have come to take our Golden Fleece!"

Medea had been hiding in the palace. She had heard her father's angry words. She ran at once to Jason and told him what the king had said.

"Come!" she cried. "We must get the Fleece and fly!"

Medea lead the Argonauts deep into the

forest where the Fleece was hidden. In the darkness, the wool shone with a golden light. Lying near it was the fierce dragon which guarded it day and night. As the heroes drew near, the dragon threw back its head and gave a mighty roar. Medea was not afraid. She walked up to the dragon and held a magic charm before its eyes. Soon the terrible monster was asleep.

Jason took the Golden Fleece from its hiding place. He ran to the ship. Medea and the other heroes followed him. They could hear the sound of the king's guards coming after them. They set sail. The ship flew over the waves like a great bird.

The wicked king sent his men after the Argonauts, but no ship was as fast as the *Argo*. The Greek heroes laughed and shouted as they watched the king's ship fall far behind.

The Argonauts had won the Golden Fleece.

⚜ PRONOUNCING INDEX ⚜